Potter's Boy

Selected Works by Tony Mitton

Wayland
The Storyteller's Secrets
The Tale of Tales
Plum

Potter's Boy

TONY MITTON

David Fickling Books

31 Beaumont Street
Oxford OX1 2NP, UK

Potter's Boy
is
A DAVID FICKLING BOOK

First published in Great Britain by
David Fickling Books,
31 Beaumont Street,
Oxford, OX1 2NP

Hardback edition published 2017
This paperback edition published 2019

Text © Tony Mitton, 2017
Cover illustration © Blacksheep-uk.com, 2017

978-1-910989-35-7

1 3 5 7 9 10 8 6 4 2

Papers used by David Fickling Books are from well-managed forests and
other responsible sources.

DAVID FICKLING BOOKS Reg. No. 8340307

A CIP catalogue record for this book is available from the British Library.

Typeset in 11½/16½pt Sabon by Falcon Oast Graphic Art Ltd.
Printed and bound in Great Britain by Clays, Ltd., Elcograf S.p.A.

For all of you . . . and for me too.
                                                    TM

'*Everything* you meet *is* the path.'

(Old Buddhist saying)

I am an old man now so it is possible I am out of tune with the times. Soon my life will be over and it will be for others to manage what becomes of the world. Already, younger people may look at me and see merely a relic, a being with little to say to the world of today.

But I have a story to tell. And I feel a need to write it down so it might stand some chance of surviving. For I believe it carries truths that should be acknowledged, things of use to people anywhere and of any time.

This story happened in the past, at a time when values and customs were different, but I believe that what may be distilled from it may still be relevant to those living now, and even those who come to be living in future times.

Bear with me. For though my style is old fashioned, you may find matter in my tale that amounts to more than mere entertainment. Like many stories there is a hero at its centre. And we are all heroes of our own stories, of course. So while at the outset you may think this hero to have little in common with yourself, as the story proceeds you may feel his experience touching you more closely than you would have imagined.

But if the words are to be written let me now begin. Let me try, as best I can, to tell you the story of the potter's boy.

Chapter One

Ryo was the son of a potter. He lived in a small hut in a remote village in the mountains of Old Chazan. His father had a little workshop to one side of the family hut. It was there he threw his pots, and nearby where he built up his kilns when it was time to fire them. He was a good potter, a skilled potter, and people came from far and wide to buy his wares. It was said that his pots had that 'special essence' that good pots should have, which made them more than just pots for everyday use. They were useful, of course. They were necessary. But they were also considered things of beauty. Some people bought them to put in their sacred alcoves, little spaces in their homes where a single vase might hold a simple branch of blossom with a piece of calligraphy above it on the wall. These alcoves were to remind them that they were a part of nature, that they were not separate from the things around them. Even the pots they used for food, drink and other purposes were made from clay, water and fire, from the natural processes of the earth they lived on, the earth from which they grew their food, the earth that supported them wherever they happened to walk. Takumi, Ryo's father, knew all this and put most of his energy into the making of pots and other clayware. The rest of his attention went into his family, into Ryo, his son. And into Emi, his wife and Hana, his daughter.

So Ryo was, in a way, fortunate. There was always food for him to eat, a warm place to live and sleep, clothes to wear and people around him that loved him. His family life was simple, but it was safe and good.

I pick up his story when he is twelve. He is just at that age when he is beginning to change from boy to man. In some ways he is still a child, but he has a growing sense of his adult life ahead of him. For some time now he has been helping his father in the workshop, learning the ways of the clay. Where it comes from, how to prepare it, how to coax a lump of clay on a wheel into becoming a pot worth putting into a kiln for firing. How to mix a glaze to paint it with. And also the beginnings of that most delicate art: how to build a kiln and set and manage a fire that will turn clay into fired and glazed ware.

His father could tell he had the skill, or rather,

the grain of rightness in him that would allow him in time to become a good potter. He might even have the makings of a great potter. But that would rely on time, work, intention and other things more difficult to predict. Besides, Takumi was a man of some wisdom. So he knew the importance of living well in the present and not setting too much store on the future. Of course, his family needed providing for. He had to be prudent. But he knew not to wish for too much, nor even to rely on too much, especially when it came to other people, who are, always and ever, unpredictable. Even those most known to us can surprise us at times with their sudden decisions and unexpected changes. So he knew that even he, Ryo's own father, who had brought Ryo up from babyhood, watching him carefully with love and caution, could not predict the course that Ryo's life would take.

Ryo's mother, Emi, was quiet, graceful and dignified. She was also fine looking, but Ryo barely noticed that. Children tend to take their homes and their parents for granted. It's simply what is, what they grow up with, what they know. How could it be anything but 'normal'? Only if things go badly, or some disaster occurs, does it occur to children to question their circumstances or their family members.

Emi looked after the home and tended a small garden behind it where she grew vegetables and a few flowers to place in the family alcove. She also kept chickens for their eggs or for meat if they stopped laying. The other thing she did, to supplement the family income, was to offer tea and rice to travellers in exchange for a few coins. A road led through the village so from time to time a traveller or two would pass through. Seeing the sign above Takumi the Potter's door they would often be glad of a rest and some tea. In summer they would sit out under the shade of the straw awning. In winter they would come into the simple front room to warm themselves by the small charcoal fire they would find burning there.

And Ryo's sister, Hana, what of her? When Ryo was twelve she was barely nine, so there was a three year gap between them. They were fond of each other. But the difference in their age and the fact of them being boy and girl was enough to create a distance between them. Ryo followed his father, while Hana stayed close to her mother. It was like that then. Boys were to be men and girls were to be women and their lives were marked out for them by that. Whether that was better than it is now I can't say. But that was how it was then, when my story takes place.

It was into this world of accepted order that the Stranger stepped. He was not expected. He just came into the village one day, like one of the many travellers who happened to pass through the village. Looking back, Ryo, his mother and his sister might think, yes, he did have a special presence, a certain dignity and composure unusual in one so humbly clad. But then in our culture, especially back then, wandering poets, hermits and sages were not so uncommon. They embraced a life of what was called 'refined poverty', which is to say that while they avoided the outer richness of material things they cultivated a kind of inner richness of heart, of spirit, of soul. In a way they were like monks, so you could call them religious. But they belonged to no order. They served no god. They were individuals who moved freely through the world, through the cosmos, as they might say, for that is how they tended to see things.

It was while the Stranger was sitting quietly in the shade of the awning, sipping a bowl of wheat tea, that the brigands arrived. They swaggered into the village with their swords and knives clinking against their armour. Their hair was long and wild, their beards were unkempt and they seemed savage and frightening. You could almost feel the village itself shrink back in terror.

There were three of them. But they occupied the space of ten. Their trade was creating fear and they did that to great effect. Their gestures were big, their voices were loud, even their facial expressions were larger than life. And they convinced any onlooker that they would do harm to anyone who came between what they wanted and what they got.

The three brigands took up a stance in the centre of the village, in the middle of the road. They looked around them ferociously. It was clear their intention was to intimidate the villagers. The biggest of the three, who seemed to be the leader, called out, turning as he spoke so as to address anyone within hearing distance.

'Bring us money and anything of value. And bring us food also. Place it on the ground in front of us. If you bring enough we will leave you unharmed until the next time we pass through. But do not keep us waiting. We are not patient men. Bring it quickly, now.'

As he finished speaking the village seemed filled with a deep silence. For a moment all was still. It was a stillness of fear and uncertainty. Nobody wanted to face the brigands. It was into this silence that a single word was heard, loud and clear, like a pebble dropped into a pond. It rang out, firm and confident, and rippled across the silent village.

'No . . . !'

There was a gasp that followed. Perhaps many villagers actually gasped out loud and what was heard was the collective gasp of many. But there was also a snarl of outrage that came from the brigands themselves.

'What?' growled the head brigand. 'Who dares defy me? Come out and fight me, if you dare.'

Nothing stirred. Nobody moved. The faintest of breezes rippled the awnings in front of the huts. And this merely exaggerated the sense of expectant hush. Who had spoken? Who had answered the brigands back with such confidence?

'Come out at once, or we shall take a villager and slay him here before you all. Come out and face us.'

A plain figure stepped lightly out across the dust road towards the brigands. Ryo realized that it was the Stranger, who had risen silently and left the shadow of their awning to confront the brigands. Ryo wanted to say, 'No, these are brigands. They will harm or kill you. They are vicious and cruel.' That is what his father had always told him. And now he wanted to pass this warning on to the Stranger. But the words stuck in his throat, and, besides, the Stranger was now standing in front of the brigands, leaving just a little distance between himself and them.

It made a strange yet vivid picture, and one that never left Ryo's memory from that time on. The three stout brigands, large and hairy and armed to the teeth with dangerous weapons. And the slight, simple figure of the plain man dressed in the ragged robe of a wanderer. It was incongruous. They seemed so unevenly matched. The brigands seemed so solid, so heavy, so powerful.

And the Stranger looked like a shadow, like the wisp of a being that might be blown away by the next breeze.

But he looked at them directly, as if unmoved, unimpressed, by their ferocity. And quite simply he repeated the one word he had spoken before, 'No.'

The head brigand's eyes widened. His jaw dropped. He turned from side to side to exchange glances with his fellows. And then he laughed. He laughed out loud from his belly.

'This is the village fool. Quite clearly this poor idiot does not know the situation he finds himself in. But we shall have to teach him a lesson anyway, if only to show the others we mean business . . .'

'No!' repeated the Stranger, this time a little louder so that all who were watching could hear it.

And now the head brigand grew angry. 'I have had enough of this foolery. You have asked for this.'

He drew his sword smoothly, with the movement of a skilled fighter. Here was a man who could handle his weapons, a professional. And yet when he cut at the Stranger's head with speed and accuracy his blade failed to meet its target and he lost his balance and stumbled clumsily. The Stranger had moved so swiftly, at the last moment, that the blade had missed. There was a murmur of surprise from the watching crowd and the brigand's two accomplices looked startled.

But the head brigand's anger was up now, and

he regained his balance and turned in fury on his adversary. He stepped towards him and cut once again with his sword. What Ryo saw next made him start with amazement and admiration. The Stranger simply made a deft sidestep, placed his foot by that of the brigand and pushed him firmly with both hands.

The brigand went down in a clatter of armour and weaponry and his sword fell from his hand. The Stranger was quick upon it and had it in his own hand in one swoop. And now he was standing with the sword at the brigand's throat, like a snake that might strike at any moment. The brigand's fellows had drawn their own blades, but the Stranger flashed them a warning glance.

'You are three, yet I can take nine before I am out-numbered. I do not advise you to enter this fight. I can read from here that you are not up to it. See, even your feet are wrongly placed. Your balance is poor.' He nodded to the nearer one, 'I could take you in three moves.' He nodded to the other, 'And you in two more. I have your measure. Do not try me.'

Ryo watched from the awning. He was rapt. The Stranger had moved with such grace, more like a dancer than a fighter. Yes, it was like watching a dance, the way the man moved with absolute precision. What did it remind him of? Ah, that was it. It was like watching the way his father's fingers could lift a lump of clay into the form of a beautiful pot or vase. It was a seemingly effortless grace that seemed to emerge from nowhere, out of nothing. Yet out of that nothing it could create something.

And now the Stranger was speaking. He was addressing the brigands. He did not shout or bully or even order them. He spoke plainly and evenly.

'Be sensible. I am one, but I can bring more. More who know how to fight like me. Do not try us. You will lose. This village is under our protection. We shall not be here but we shall be listening. If we hear of any harm that comes to this village from your hands we shall be upon you. And we will come quietly, by stealth, from the shadows. You will not hear us until our knives are at your throats. You will be safe nowhere. This is a warning, not a threat. Mend your ways. Try to make a more honest living. Those who live by the sword soon die by the sword. Stay out of trouble.'

'Who are you?' murmured one of the brigands uneasily. 'Where have you come from?'

'Some call us "the Hidden Ones". You would be hard pressed to find us. But you might meet us any-where, as today. Now take your weapons and go. Put them to better use than frightening poor, hardworking villagers.'

The brigands did not look happy. They had been shamed in front of the whole village and they were still shaken by their encounter with fighting skill far greater than theirs. They felt foolish. Everyone watched them as they shuffled off out of the village, muttering quietly as they went.

As they disappeared around the bend in the road people turned to find the Stranger, to thank him and to honour him. But he had gone. He seemed to have slipped away while they were watching the retreating figures of the three brigands.

Ryo looked the other way, to see if he could see the Stranger heading off in the other direction, along the single road that led through the village. But he was not there. Odd. Ah, the hill track, he thought. He has taken the hill track. How did he know about that? Only the villagers know that track. How did he find it?

Ryo slipped through the gap between two huts and was off up the hill track at speed. His feet knew this track. He could run it with his eyes shut, and had done in a game he'd played with the other village children when younger. But today his eyes were wide open and scanning for a glimpse of the Stranger.

And then he saw him. That slight, lithe figure, so plainly dressed, so nondescript, climbing the winding track up the hill. Who would have guessed that any-body, but especially a nobody like that, could contain such skill and power? He could have been any traveller, on any day, on any track.

13

'Hey, mister! Wait for me. Please stop!' Ryo heard his voice call out before he had even planned what he intended to say or do.

The figure paused for the briefest moment, then went on walking up the track.

'Mister, please. It's me, the potter's son. From the village where you stopped for tea. Please stop for a moment.'

The figure halted and turned slowly to take in the sight of the young boy coming up the track towards him. He waited in silence, still. Ryo also paused for a moment. Now that the Stranger had stopped Ryo suddenly realized he did not quite know what he was going to say to him. He only knew that he had to discover more about this man, this stranger, about where he came from, about how he could do what he could do . . . Yes, that was it. Ryo wanted to know where he could learn such skills. Ryo wanted to know and own such power as he'd seen this man wield. Ryo wanted to be like him. How could this be achieved? Where could he go to learn? What must he do?

Ryo's thoughts were in a whirl. So he just blurted out the first words that came into his mind. 'Take me with you. Teach me to be like you. Show me. I am young. I am smart. I can learn . . .'

The man looked down at Ryo. He did not smile. It was as if he was taking the earnest young boy's words seriously. He looked into Ryo's eyes for a few moments before he spoke. 'You cannot come with me. I can take you nowhere. You belong in the village and you have a family. If I let you come with me, and I cannot do that, but if I did, your parents would worry. They might think that the brigands had taken you, out of revenge. And besides, you are not ready. You have only the clothes you stand up in. And what's more, you are too young. How old are you?'

'I'm twelve, see. Nearly a man. I'm not a child any more. It's almost time for me to seek my way in life. And today, when I saw you deal with the brigands, I knew, I realized. I thought to myself, "That's my way. That's what I want to be and do. I want to be a fighter like that."' Ryo paused and waited for an answer.

'Fighting is not a good way,' said the man thoughtfully. 'It leads to a life of loneliness and takes you to bad places where there is unhappiness, misery, grief. Your father is a potter. You could be a potter like him. That is a good life, a rich life, a rewarding life, a life of making things and bringing pleasure and meaning to people. That is so much better a life than that of a fighter. A good potter is valued by his people.'

'But so is a hero,' Ryo said quickly. 'And I should like to be a hero, like you.'

'Listen,' said the Stranger decisively. 'You cannot come with me. Do not even think to try. You know my skill. I can easily outwit you. I can make myself disappear into the undergrowth so you can never find me. I shall go on. And you shall go back to your village. And you will probably never see me again.'

'But I shall never forget you,' said Ryo certainly. 'And when I am older I shall find a way to learn to be like you. Somewhere there must be someone who can teach me such things as you know. I will find them and learn. One day I will be like you.'

'Well,' said the man. And a sigh entered his voice, a sense of surrender. As if, perhaps, he had heard the note of true earnestness in this young lad. 'All right. If you are determined, listen and remember. I will say it once. Leave it a year. Until you are beyond thirteen. Then, if your parents permit, pack yourself a travelling bundle with clothes and food. And go to Cold Mountain. Look for the Hermit. If you find him, tell him what you want, if you still want it. If you can't find him, return home and learn to be a potter, for that would probably be the better way for you. But you will do what you will do. That is for you to decide.

'Now let me go. I have a journey to make and a promise to keep. I must be on my way. Go back to the village before your people start to worry about you. They have had a shock. You should be with them. Go and be with your family. Go now.'

The man's words were so clear, so firm, and his

manner was so certain, that Ryo knew he had to obey. As the man turned, they glanced at one another and Ryo felt as if something special passed between them, as if their lives were somehow now linked. It was a strange feeling, an intuition. There was no proof to be had. But Ryo felt that today his life had changed, had turned a corner. It was as if things would never be the same again for him. Was this what they called 'growing up'? Or was it something else? Something less usual? Something distinct? He couldn't know. But it was a different Ryo who turned back to his village from the eager young boy who had run out in pursuit of the Stranger. He had run out desperately, swiftly. His return was slow and thoughtful. When he got home his people were relieved to see him safe. But they saw no difference in him.

CHAPTER TWO

As time passed his parents did, however, note a difference in his behaviour, in his demeanour. His mother found him less childish, slower and more thoughtful. Moody at times. His father found he seemed distracted, less eager to learn the ways of the clay and the kiln. And often daydreaming when he should have been attending to the tasks at hand in the pottery.

'I am a little worried about Ryo,' said Emi to her husband. 'He seems sad, dreamy, not himself. It's since the brigands came to the village that day. Perhaps the fright has unbalanced him. Perhaps he is haunted by fear now. This can happen to people after a bad scare.'

'He is growing,' said Takumi. 'When young boys grow into men it takes time. Their bodies change, their minds change. There is much happening to them. Sometimes it drives them inward. They can be moody. Let him be. Things will improve as time passes. Time will do the job that we cannot do by interfering.'

Emi nodded. 'Yes, in a few years our little Hana will grow into a woman. And that too will bring changes and not be easy. Good parents take things one day at a time. We must be patient and steady.'

But one day Ryo lost his temper in the workshop. A pot he was drawing up between finger and thumb, while working the wheel with his foot, went askew. He snatched it up and hurled it out of the open doorway in his rage. 'Oh, bloody, bloody, bloody pots and clay,' he yelled and stamped. 'Oh, bloody damn them all . . .'

His father was across the workshop and upon him in a trice. He grabbed Ryo's wrist to stop him doing further damage and placed his other hand firmly on Ryo's shoulder. He looked down intensely into Ryo's eyes as if searching for an explanation.

'What's this?' he demanded. 'What is this all about? Have you taken leave of your senses? This is our workplace. This is our livelihood. You do not take your anger out on what brings us our living. What are you thinking of?'

'It's just, it's just . . .' muttered Ryo helplessly. But his words dried up on him and his anger blocked him from expressing himself. So he fell silent and looked at the floor, feeling his cheeks grow hot and his eyes blur with tears he did not wish to allow to fall.

'Go and sit by the stream, in the quiet place,' said his father in a calmer voice. 'Go and collect yourself. When you have gathered your thoughts and your feelings we will talk. Maybe then you can tell me what the matter is.'

The stream that ran through the village passed below the potter's hut where a small tree grew, giving shade. There was a large flat stone there where Ryo's father, Takumi, often went to sit quietly to watch the waters as they passed. He had taught Ryo as a little child how soothing it could be to do just that. To sit and gaze at the swirling, twirling waters as they flowed by in their silvery way, making patterns that formed and dissolved as you watched. If you watched long enough, sometimes the same patterns would re-form before disappearing once again. Once or twice, when he was still quite young, he had heard his father murmuring to himself. What was he saying? 'It is like time, like life . . .' Or something like that. Ryo had never understood what that meant, but he often remembered the words when he found himself near the rock and the water.

Now Ryo was here again. This time angry, trembling, frustrated and ashamed. No longer a child, but not yet a man. In between. And feeling vexed and strange. He was tired of the pots, the clay, this quiet village where little happened. The brigands coming had been frightening, it was true. But at least it had been an event. At least it had shaken the dull old place up a bit. And it had introduced him to the thrill and excitement of seeing the Stranger in action, weaving rings of invisible confusion around the clumsy brigands with their awkward weapons. Ah, yes, the Stranger. He was never far from Ryo's imagination. Ryo even dreamed of him at times. In his dreams the two of them would be dealing with a whole band of brigands, ducking, dodging, disarming and confusing the slow, baffled, heavy men weighed down with their armour and weaponry. The two of them would perform their brave dance together and the dream would end with them both flying through the air onto a rooftop to laugh at their defeated opponents.

But that was a dream. Whereas this was real life. And now he had upset his father by behaving badly. He was ashamed. He knew this was not the way to do things. But he had been battling with himself, bottling up his feelings because he knew he might not be able to have his way. The Stranger had tried to dissuade him. And he feared his father would do the same. But he did not want to hear his father's words on the matter, because while he thought his father would oppose and prevent him, he knew he would be unable to give up the fantasy of going off to become one of the Hidden Ones.

He would have to talk to his father now. For he had

shown his rage and behaved badly so he would have to account for himself somehow. Better to tell the truth, thought Ryo. To pretend or conceal would just make things more difficult for him as time passed. Now that he had let his feelings burst out it would be better to speak from his heart, to tell things as they truly were for him. At least he would then find out where he stood.

CHAPTER THREE

'I want to be like the Stranger,' said Ryo. 'I want to learn to be one of the Hidden Ones . . .' He could hardly believe it. As the words came out of his mouth it was as if someone else was speaking and he was simply hearing the words form in the air. Was he actually saying this to his father? Was this another of his dreams? No, this was reality, sure enough. His father had sat down quietly with him, just the two of them, under the tree by the stream. And Takumi had not been aggressive or punitive in any way. True, Ryo had behaved badly and broken one of the basic rules of the workshop, never to move or act in any way likely to cause damage to the delicate or fragile things being made there. But Ryo's outburst had been so extreme and out of character that this was clearly an unusual situation, a situation beyond the normal rules. And therefore a situation in which standard discipline should not apply.

He expected his father to stop him there. He expected him to interrupt, to tell him that this was some crazy notion or childish dream. He paused, waiting to hear his father tell him about the pleasures and virtues of pottery, of ceramic work, of all the skills and joys to be worked for and won in that fine and honourable trade. But he did not. He just nodded thoughtfully.

'Go on,' he said. 'Tell me more.'

So Ryo told him about what he had felt when he had seen the Stranger move into action before the brigands. He told his father how transfixed he had been by the grace, by the beauty, of the Stranger's movements. How it had seemed more like dancing than like fighting. How, yes, this was odd, since the brigands were men of violence who were heavily armed and meant him real harm. And yet how he had somehow seemed above all that, so much so that he had not troubled to punish them in any way, but had left fear and warning to do their work if they would. But what Ryo wanted to get across to his father was the intense excitement he had felt in seeing what the Stranger could actually do with his body, with his movements, with his timing and skill. He, Ryo, felt that if he started now, when young, he might one day be able to command such skill himself, if only he could find someone to teach him.

'But,' said Ryo despondently to Takumi, 'there is surely no one in the village, nor near it, who could teach me such things. And the Stranger has moved on. It is unlikely he will ever return here. And I am a potter's son. And it is my destiny to become a potter as you are in due course. Yet I feel somehow cut out to be like the Stranger, not to be a potter as my father is . . .'

As his voice trailed away he gazed down into the swirling waters and there was a short period of silence as both he and his father looked thoughtfully into the moving stream. Then, slowly, ruminatively, as if searching among the ripples for the right thing, for the truest way, Takumi began to speak. He was speaking to Ryo, but it was also as if he was talking to the waters below them, to the air around them and to himself too. It was almost, the odd thought occurred to Ryo, as if Takumi was trying to let the truth speak through him, rather than giving his personal opinion.

'My father was not a potter,' said Takumi. 'So, you see, I too chose a different way for myself when I was young. My father was a farmer, as you know. Quite a rich farmer, with land, and with other people working for him. And he expected me to take on the farm from him as he grew older, to take his place when he died. But in my village then there was a potter, a very fine potter, and as a child I used to watch him at work and I came to learn the ways of the clay simply by observing him with fascination. He even began to let me play with the clay after a while, and eventually to show me how to shape it with my fingers. I began to dream of being a potter like him one day. The desire in me began to grow to make my own pots and ceramics until that was all I really wanted. The thought of being a farmer filled me with a kind of dull dread and gave me a heavy heart. But I was fortunate. My father was a wise and thoughtful man, a fair man. So, when it was time, he let me have my way. When my sister married, he passed the farm onto her and her husband, leaving me free to take up an apprenticeship with the potter.'

Takumi paused from his tale, bringing himself back from his past to this present, beside the stream, beneath the tree, sitting on the flat stone with his own son, looking at the turning, twisting waters as they flowed by.

'So you see, I am honour bound to be with you as he was with me. To listen to the voice of your heart and to respect it if it is truly sincere. And it seems so to me. As you talk about the effect of the Stranger upon your heart and mind, you remind me of the effect the potter had on me, all those years ago, when my own future lay ahead of me like a path untrodden, as yours does for you now.'

Ryo almost held his breath. He could not quite believe what he was hearing. His father went on.

'If you truly, deeply feel that what you think you wish is the right way for you, then you must do it. There may be some uncertainty in you. You cannot be sure that you will be great at what you attempt, or even successful. But there comes a point where the best thing is simply to try yourself out, to put yourself as far towards what you intend as you can and to allow fate, chance or fortune to do the rest. That is the best that any of us can do.'

Seizing his chance, Ryo cut in. 'The Stranger did leave me with a suggestion. He said that when I had passed thirteen, and I am about to do that very soon, I should pack a travelling bundle and go to Cold Mountain to seek the Hermit. That is all he said. But he gave me the name of a place to go and a person to look for. That is a start. Would you allow me to do that? Would you give a father's permission?'

'Your mother will find this difficult,' said Takumi. 'I shall not find it easy myself, seeing you go off to seek a life of your own, away from the family. And of course your sister will miss you. She looks up to you as her older brother, and I know she admires you. So your leaving will create a hole in the family. We will feel your absence sharply. But we cannot allow that to hold you back from finding your true future. To make you stay with us would just create unhappiness, first for you, and in turn for all of us. So, yes. I grant you a father's permission to go and choose your own way for the future. Do as you must.'

They sounded formal, those last words of his father's. But then they were a formality, of course. To make it bind, Takumi had to state it formally, matter of factly. It was, after all, a tradition, the way it had to be done. Back then, in the village, the old ways still held. Now things are different, of course. But back then things had to be done a certain way. And everyone knew what that way was. There was good and bad to it. But things change. Which brings gains and losses. New ground is found, old ground is lost. It is nearly always so. Sometimes we miss the best of the old ways. Sometimes we are glad of the improvements of the new ways. But time passes and things change. And there is no going back.

So now it was done. Ryo was to go. And he wanted to. As the time approached he felt misgivings. Uneasiness sometimes clawed at the pit of his stomach. Sometimes his heart stirred with sadness at the thought of leaving his family behind. And he even began to find a certain comfort in the dullness of the old village, and a strong fondness for the place in which he had grown up. But none of that persuaded him to change his mind. He must go to Cold Mountain to seek the Hermit.

Chapter Four

When the day came it was a quiet departure. Ryo's bundle was packed and he had a staff to protect himself with, in case of difficulty or danger. His father had asked around the village for directions towards Cold Mountain. One of the old men of the village turned out once to have been there, to help carry some goods to a settlement that lay near its foot. So Ryo now had verbal directions, which should prove enough. A mountain should not be easy to miss, even in an area where there were many.

Ryo's mother held him tightly for a moment. Then she kissed his forehead. Ryo in turn kissed Hana's forehead. And then his father hugged him before looking into his face.

'Take care,' he said. 'And do your best.' He paused. 'You are always welcome here. This is your family home. Come and see us when you get the chance. We will always be glad to see you.'

They watched his figure walking away down the road and out of the village. Many of the villagers had heard of his departure, and stood in the doorways or under their awnings to see him go and to wish him well in the traditional way. Each one murmured the words, 'Be well and be safe,' as they raised a hand in farewell. And soon he was gone from the village and out of sight.

The journey took him three days of steady walking. For the two nights that he was on the road he found warm, safe places to wrap himself in his blanket. Screened from view by foliage he slept well enough, falling asleep with the thickening dusk and waking at first light so as to use maximum daylight for walking. He passed through three villages on his way, one on each day of his journey. He paused to ask directions, making sure his way was true, and in one of the villages accepted hospitality in the form of tea and hot rice.

As he sipped the welcome hot tea from the tea bowl his host asked him where he was bound.

'I'm headed for Cold Mountain, sir,' he replied simply.

'Cold Mountain?' said his host with a note of enquiry in his voice, and a slight hint of astonishment. 'Why should you wish to go *there*?'

'I am going to meet the Hermit,' said Ryo.

'The Hermit?!' exclaimed his host, unable to conceal his surprise.

'Yes,' said Ryo. 'Do you know him?'

'Know him?' repeated his host with amusement at what was clearly a fanciful idea. 'Well, of course I have heard of him. But no one I know has ever met him, nor even seen him. I rather thought he was more of a legend than a person.'

'No, I think he is really there. I think he exists,' said Ryo. 'I was told to seek him out. So I am now on my way to find him.'

'Well,' said his host. 'If you find him, let me know, should you be passing this way. And good luck to you. If you fail in your search, do call on me on your way back. You are welcome to rest here on your journey again. A boy with a purpose should be encouraged. Your determination is admirable.'

After a rest and some conversation in which Ryo told his host of his family and his village he set off, secure in the sense he was headed for Cold Mountain and should be there by the end of the day. He had not told his host of his exact purpose for he was somehow shy to talk of such a thing. It might sound presumptuous, overambitious, or even overly idealistic. Certainly to another person. But Ryo was not another person. He was himself. And he felt determined to test this ambition he found in himself. It would not go away and he sensed that if he did not deal with it practically, through action, then it would continue to cause him trouble and brew unhappiness in him.

Towards the end of the day Ryo began to see the shape of Cold Mountain through the mist. From then it was as if the mountain revealed itself gradually to him, shifting bit by bit from a vague ghost into a very clear reality. Once he could see it from close up he noticed that it seemed to form a world of its own. At its foot it was swathed in forest. Further up it seemed to be crinkled with contours creating all kinds of concealed spaces, clearings, inlets where shelter might be found or made. Further up still it became wild and bare, a place where few people would find reason to go and where few animals would find sustenance. A place, thought Ryo, where the dragons of air might be found sleeping, should anyone dare to venture a visit.

When he reached the foot of the mountain he circled it until he found a path leading into the dense forest. He paused first, preparing to be cautious and watchful as he penetrated this place. He made sure his bundle was firmly strapped to his back, leaving his hands free to wield his staff in the event of meeting an aggressive beast of some kind. Perhaps a wild pig or some such. Then he followed the path into the wood, hoping soon to come out onto the more open part of the mountain.

He was nervous, but he took a deep breath and forced himself forward, step by step.

He heard rustlings as he went through the wood, but nothing approached him. Probably, he thought, most creatures would be more wary of him than he of them, what with his human-smell. Perhaps so few people came through here that he represented the unknown to them, something unfamiliar to be avoided. And yet there was a path. To remain open it must at times be trodden, or at least kept clear for passage by someone. Could that be the Hermit?

When he emerged from the forest he was surprised to find it still quite light in the space beyond. But then dusk had not yet thickened, and up here the light would remain longer in the sky, he realized.

So now he was on the mountain. And now he had to find the Hermit. 'Find the Hermit.' It almost sounded like some strange, magical quest or puzzle. What did it remind him of, the phrase, 'Finding the Hermit' . . . ? That was it, the phrase they used in the village to denote something impossibly difficult, 'Riding the Dragon'. As a boy he had imagined doing just that: Riding the Dragon. He had seen himself in his mind's eye, astride the writhing, scaled, flying serpent, holding onto the base of its wings as it coiled around clouds and rode the currents of the air. But that was a heroic image, whereas right now he was plodding round a deserted mountainside looking for signs of a strange old man. That did not, somehow, seem very heroic to Ryo.

Yet he had travelled hard to get here. And he'd had to persuade his parents to allow him to let go of their expectations of him becoming a potter like his father. And he'd had to follow the Stranger out of the village and to press him to give him some pointer, some direction, something to reach towards in order to become someone skilled in . . . what was it? Fighting?

Even back then, though he had not formulated it, Ryo balked at the word 'fighting'. It did not somehow do justice to what he had witnessed in the encounter between the Stranger and the three brigands. There was more to it than that. It was not simply 'fighting'. There was some inner quality at work in the Stranger's actions that was more than simply physical skill and practised movement. There was a quality of mind, spirit, heart, feeling . . . or perhaps a mix of those things. He thought of the word he had learned from his parents, 'hsin'. It meant 'heart', but it meant 'mind' also. Not either, but both, a kind of blend of the two. And where was *hsin* located in the body? Where could it be found? Could you find it by opening up the body of a dead person? Probably not. Like a ghost, it might by then have fled the corpse. But it probably lived somewhere between the head and the heart, at least from the point of view of the imagination. Ryo began to feel almost dizzy. Thinking about *hsin* always seemed to have that effect on him. 'Don't worry about it,' his father had said to him. 'It will look after itself. The harder you seek it the further you will be from it. Try to do the right thing at the right time and *hsin* will be peaceful inside you.'

That was it! That was what Ryo had seen, or sensed, in the Stranger. A quality of peace inside him. Although he was swiftly active it was all carried out with a kind of detached grace, without anger or ugly aggression. The brigands had seemed powerful and strong, but they were bullies, pushing out arrogance, almost seeming to brag in the way they stood or moved. Whereas the Stranger was quiet and humble in his stance. Almost self-effacing, yet confident and unafraid. Fronting up to whatever might happen next. Ready to move in accordance with it. Not reacting. But alert and responsive. Back then, Ryo did not have the words for such things. These are my words, now, as I tell you my story. Ryo, of course, had not such language. But he sensed the existence and the influence of the qualities the Stranger showed. And he wanted to reach towards them with the natural youthful ambition and eagerness that a healthy young person will feel. He grasped something of these things in his raw, untutored way.

Ryo came out of his thoughts to find he'd stumbled into a clearing of levelled ground. He had been so taken up with his thinking that he'd been walking automatically along the path he was on, not really attending to the path itself, absorbed in his own interior world of memory and rumination. But now he had arrived somewhere. There were clear signs of habitation.

Ahead of him he saw a simple rustic hut, such as the poorer folk in the villages constructed for themselves. It looked like the dwelling of a single person. There was room enough in it, judging by its size, for one person to live modestly in a frugal way. But for all its simplicity it had a look of refinement about it. While it was made of basic, natural materials, it was made with care, by someone who had worked methodically to make the best of the crude materials they had to hand. Whoever had made this hut was a person of skill and discernment. Ryo was the son of a fine potter. His father had trained him so he had an eye for such things. He knew craft when he saw it.

There were two other small structures. One looked as if it was a storeroom for keeping kindling wood and charcoal and materials for mending the huts when necessary, things that someone must have gathered in advance for when they might be needed. The other appeared to be empty. Perhaps it was accommodation for guests, for travellers being offered hospitality or overnight lodging. Not far from the main hut, on the levelled ground in front of it, was an open fire that was still smouldering. A few cooking pots stood near to it and there was a contraption over it for hanging pots above the flames and adjusting them to the required height.

Yet Ryo could see no person there. Whoever lived here was for the moment out of sight, if not away elsewhere. It seemed likely that this person would have some knowledge of the Hermit. This itself might be the Hermit's home, his settlement. But if it wasn't, then surely anyone living here would have met him or know of his whereabouts. Cold Mountain was a large area, but seemed almost entirely unpopulated. Anyone living here for any length of time would be sure to be aware of other inhabitants, even if just as distant neighbours.

Ryo decided the best course of action would be to stay and wait for the return of whoever happened to live here. This was a wild, deserted place and here, at least, was some kind of homestead, some human presence. And the dusk was drawing in. His best chance was to wait here and hope to be allowed to sleep within the cleared area. If he was lucky, in one of the huts, or perhaps near to the embers of the fire, wrapped in his blanket on the ground. Maybe he would be offered tea or food of some kind. And conversation would be welcome. His mind went back to his family and for a moment he could see them there in his mind's eye, his sister helping his mother prepare the evening meal, his father bringing kindling or charcoal in to feed the small central hearth that warmed the little hut he knew so well. For a moment he was overwhelmed by a wave of sadness, a longing to be back there with them in the familiar warmth and with people who loved him.

He pulled himself together. Such feelings would not help him. It was time to grow up. He had a purpose. He must remind himself of that. He had not come all this way only to back off now and go slouching back home with his tail between his legs. He must take feelings like this as a test of his resolve. Yes. He must be brave, and bravery sometimes consisted simply of staying put and waiting. 'There's a time to act and a time to wait.' It had stuck in his head. One of his father's sayings. He'd said it to Ryo when they were tending the kiln to fire the pots. But Ryo knew it referred to more than just pots.

This is someone's home, thought Ryo. I can't simply bed down here uninvited. That would be rude. Yet I can't bring myself to go back and sleep on the mountainside either. The forest below seems an unsafe place to sleep. There may be snakes or wild creatures that could do me harm in the dark. What should I do?

He realized that the best thing would be to wrap himself in his blanket and prop himself up against a small tree that grew on the edge of the clearing. That way he might be comfortable and at rest while able to stay awake until the inhabitant of the settlement returned home, which surely they must do before dark. Being close to the embers of the fire and the sight of the huts would comfort Ryo and make him feel less in the wilderness, less at the mercy of wild nature. Yes, that would be the best thing to do for now. There was a small stream running close to the clearing, so Ryo cupped his hands and took a drink from it. Then he placed his bundle beside him, lay down his staff and wrapped himself in his blanket, determining to wait and see what fate would bring his way. At his back the small tree supported him and its canopy of foliage overhead felt like a roof sheltering him from the vastness of the evening sky.

Despite his best efforts to stay awake he was soon dreaming. In his dream he was roaming over a deserted mountain top, searching. A voice in his ears kept chanting, 'Seek the Hermit, seek the Hermit . . .' But there was nowhere sensible to look. Suddenly, in the sky above him, he saw a dragon of air emerge from behind a white cloud. Its scales flashed as they caught the light and it turned and coiled in the sky above him. He had nowhere to hide and it soon caught sight of him and flew down to hover above him. It stared at him fiercely, plumes of vapour curling from its flared nostrils. Ryo stared back in awe and terror. He opened his mouth to speak, to try to reason with it, to tell it that he meant no harm or disrespect, but no sound would come from his lungs, from his throat. No words could be squeezed up out of him.

He came to, to discover that there was indeed someone standing over him, looking down from above, curiously, into his face. But this was no dragon. It was an old man. He was dressed in simple clothes: black trousers, straw sandals and a black tunic jacket of coarse material. He could be a peasant or a monk, by his look. It was hard to say which. But though old he looked alert and in good health. His gaze was keen. And he was well groomed. What hair he had left was short and his face bore a light, white stubble.

It took Ryo a moment or so to transfer from his dream to reality. At first he was startled, as one can be on waking suddenly. Briefly he did not know who or what or where he was. For a second or so he overlaid the image of the dragon onto the old man, so saw him as a dark presence looming above him. But as his dream dissolved he could see there was no threat. The old man was simply waiting for Ryo to wake up so that he might address him. And perhaps he was reading him in advance, taking him in by assessing his clothes, his looks and the baggage beside him.

'Oh, um, er, forgive me . . .' mumbled Ryo, trying to gather his wits. He had been weary from his day's walking and had fallen asleep quite understandably.

But he had hoped to be awake and in possession of himself when the occupant of the clearing returned. He had wanted to make a good impression, especially if this turned out to be the Hermit himself. Being asleep in a heap under a tree was not the way he had intended to introduce himself.

The man stepped back, allowing Ryo to pull himself together and stand up in order to regain his dignity and also to show respect to an elder. Once Ryo was on his feet and had bowed formally to the man, a gesture which was returned to him, though less deeply, the man spoke to him. His voice was clear and level, neither over-friendly nor hostile.

'Who are you? What brings you here? Are you lost?'

Ryo did his best to answer these questions clearly. 'My name is Ryo. I come from the village of Furukawa, the village of the Old River, about three days' walk from here. I was told to come to Cold Mountain to seek the Hermit. I stumbled into this clearing a while ago but nobody was here. So I sat down to wait for someone to ask. And then, forgive me, I fell asleep.' Ryo looked a little ashamed to admit that. But he persisted, 'Can you tell me? Do you know the Hermit of Cold Mountain? Does he live nearby? How can I find him? A villager half a day from here said the Hermit was just a legend. Have I come on a fool's errand? Did I misunderstand? Am I seeking a ghost or some kind of folktale?'

The old man put up his hand to stop the flow of Ryo's babbled questions. When Ryo fell silent he spoke again, slowly and clearly, in a steady, measured way.

'I am Unzen. This, here, is my home. There is no hermit I know of on Cold Mountain, unless that is supposed to describe me. So perhaps whoever told you to come here meant you to come to me. I cannot say for sure. Tell me more about this person. How did you come to meet them and what led them to direct you here to find this so-called hermit?'

Again he put up a hand, this time to delay Ryo's answers. 'But you are weary and you've travelled far. Come and sit near the fire and I will make tea to refresh you as you tell me your story. And do not worry about your lodging for tonight. Cold Mountain is a bleak place to sleep out and there are no other dwellings here. You will sleep in the guest hut. It will be dry and warm there and you will be safe.'

The old man led Ryo over to where the embers of the fire still glowed dully. He pointed to a piece of hewn wood to indicate where Ryo should sit. Ryo put down his staff and bundle and sat on the low stool, placing his knees on the ground with his feet behind him. From this position he watched as Unzen refreshed the fire. He poured fresh water into the metal kettle and swung it above the heat. From the main hut he fetched a small tray with a rough clay teapot, a metal caddy, two tea bowls and a bamboo stirring strip. The water would take some time to boil. So in the meantime Unzen settled himself on his own wooden stool, looked directly at Ryo and said simply, 'So, tell me your story. What brings you here . . . ?'

Chapter Five

As Ryo told his story he noticed how attentively the old man was listening to him. From time to time he nodded and just occasionally he let out an 'Ah . . .' or a 'Yes . . .' without interrupting Ryo but confirming that he was understanding what was being said. Occasionally he refilled Ryo's tea bowl with the hot wheat tea he'd brewed. When he did this Ryo paused ceremoniously, as was the custom, holding his tea bowl forward and nodding in thanks when it was full.

As Ryo drew to the end of his story Unzen leaned forward and banked up the fire. Ryo waited to hear what his response would be.

'I know this man who sent you here. You are right. I *am* the hermit he spoke of. And this *is* the Cold Mountain he meant you to seek out. I am sure the man you describe in your story is Akio. It can only be him from what you tell. And probably only he would have suggested you coming here . . .' He let his voice trail off as he gazed thoughtfully into the warm embers of the fire. Then he resumed.

'But it is late and you will be tired. For now, sleep would be the best thing. In the morning we will talk again when you are fresh and full of purpose. Then, perhaps, you will know your own mind more clearly. And also I may be able to advise you more wisely. Let us sleep on it.'

He showed Ryo to a little lean-to at the edge of the clearing where he could wash and relieve himself before sleep. After that Ryo made his way to the guest hut where he found a rough bed filled with sweet smelling dry grasses which served as a mattress. Wrapping himself in his blanket and settling himself with a tired sigh he was soon fast asleep.

When he woke the next day it felt as if he'd barely been asleep for a few minutes, so deeply had he slept. But he was refreshed and he gazed with pleasure at the clear light shining in the doorway to his hut. He rose from his bed and stretched like a cat, as he always did on rising. Then he went to the doorway to see out.

At the far side of the clearing, on a patch of levelled dry earth, the old man was moving about in a strange way, as if dancing. But if this was the case then he was dancing to an inner music. His breath seemed deep and measured and his movements made it appear as if they were happening in slow motion. From time to time his balance shifted from one foot to the other while the free leg moved through the air to find its next point of contact with the earth. His hands and arms drew into his body, sometimes forming gestures, sometimes pushing outwards as if thrusting away an invisible opponent or partner or force. Unzen's body would twist and turn, facing in a range of directions. It was as if his centre was a pivot or axis around which all his movements took place, or from which they all flowed.

Then suddenly, as Ryo watched, he was moving at four times the speed, or even more. The tension had increased and his swiftness was uncanny and surprising, especially for a man of his age. And then he was back into the slow, steady, breathing rhythm of before. He drew himself back into a standing position, gave a brief, curt bow with his hands together as if in prayer, or what Ryo would have called *gassho*, and then seemed to step out of an imaginary bubble and back into the ordinary world of everyday movement. He took in the sight of Ryo watching from the doorway and raised his hand amicably to him.

'A little every day, to start each day, just to keep myself in condition. The habit of a lifetime. When one drops such things one begins to die much faster.

But now it's time for breakfast. Let's eat. We'll eat in silence. Then we'll talk.'

Ryo had already noticed how Unzen spoke in a way that seemed to state the obvious. As if there was a predetermined, right way to do standard things. It might have sounded bossy, coming from anybody else. But when Unzen spoke it was more like declaring the natural order of things. Ryo found it strangely restful, relieving him of the need to ask questions, or even to exercise 'good manners'. Things somehow seemed to flow naturally around Unzen. It was noticeable to Ryo and impressed him.

When they had eaten a simple breakfast of millet porridge, water and wheat tea, Unzen addressed Ryo directly and formally.

'So, you wish to learn the skills you saw in Akio when he confronted the brigands in your village . . .'

Ryo nodded earnestly.

Unzen continued. 'Such things are not learned swiftly. They are not mere tricks and techniques. To learn such things requires great commitment, strong dedication and endless practice. It is not so much a training as a lifetime, a life-commitment. Are you sure you have the determination to make such an undertaking? Is there fire in your heart and a strong wind in your mind for such a thing?'

That last was a strange question, yet Ryo sensed

its meaning. He felt he could indeed feel such forces in himself. It would be a question of harnessing and training them. So he nodded vehemently. 'Yes, sir, yes. I believe there is . . .'

'Not enough to believe. Believe is weak. Believe is of the small mind that witters and thinks and plays with words. Necessary to feel and sense. Emotion, sensation, not just thought. And even something deeper than those. Can you detect a deep purpose in yourself for this quest?'

Ryo paused. Then he replied, 'I am thirteen years old, coming fourteen. I have left my home and journeyed here alone. I have found you, using just a few words. Does that prove nothing?'

Suddenly Unzen laughed at the boy's seriousness. 'Ah, I ask too much too soon. Forgive me. It has been a long time since I've had to consider such things. You can stay if you wish. Then, as and when you seem ready, I may teach you some of what I know. I may be able to pass on some of what I have mastered. I warn you in advance, it is not an easy business. It is not a simple process.'

And so the matter was decided. Ryo was allowed to stay. Gradually, as Unzen thought fit, he would train Ryo in some of the skills he had come to learn. For a while, Ryo could hardly believe that his journey had begun, that he was beginning his training as a . . . what exactly was it? A warrior? A fighter? He would have to wait to find out. And even then there might not be a known word for it. But soon all such thoughts dropped aside as he was kept busy just living with Unzen from day to day, from hour to hour and even from minute to minute.

Chapter Six

The first stage of Ryo's training was simply to learn to do things 'properly', as Unzen put it. His duties consisted of learning to maintain the settlement they were living in, to do all the things necessary in order to live a decent and healthy life in a forest clearing, half-way up a mountainside. To Ryo this seemed to have very little to do with fighting or warrior skills, but more like learning to be a personal servant to Unzen. But Unzen was the master and the only source of the skills Ryo hoped to acquire. So what else could he do but buckle down and do as he was told? Perhaps that was part of the process?

Curiously, Unzen showed a keen interest in the way that Ryo did just ordinary things. For instance, Ryo was carrying the wooden bucket filled with water from the stream. It was heavy and the water slopped over its sides, wetting Ryo's feet and the ground where it fell.

'Stop. Wait,' Unzen intervened, crossing the clearing towards him.

'Look. Watch.' Unzen took the bucket from him and showed him how to hold it a better way. He took a few steps and Ryo could see that Unzen's grip, and the way he held the bucket in relation to his body, resulted in the pane of water remaining stable as he walked.

'Also look at my feet, my legs . . .'

Ryo watched as Unzen took a few more steps in slow motion, to demonstrate more clearly how his posture and his gait affected the stability of the bucket of water as it moved through space while being carried.

'Do you see . . . ? Now, you try.' Unzen watched as Ryo tried to imitate his grasp and gait.

'Good, better. But more like this.' Unzen corrected Ryo's grip and bent down to shift his foot into a more stable position. Ryo could feel the difference.

There were many examples of such moments in Ryo's daily life in the weeks that followed. It was as if Unzen was retraining him to move in ways that were more focused, more conscious. At times it reminded him of the way his father had trained him to handle and shape clay in the pottery shed. Unzen was bringing such close attention to every movement or task, no matter how small and apparently trivial. Now it was buckets and brooms. Perhaps later it would be swords and staves?

But there came a time, a few months into his training, when Ryo began to feel an exasperation, an impatience, with his daily life on the mountain.

I came here to be like Akio, he began to muse. But I am more like a serving maid in a farmer's kitchen. Where is the dignity in this? Where is the honour I hoped for? Why is Unzen not teaching me the skills of fighting? Is this a trick whereby he gets an obedient servant? Am I just a convenience to him?

He put this to Unzen in a quiet moment by the fire, as they were sipping tea. Of course he questioned tactfully, trying to conceal any sign of impatience or irritation. But Unzen could sense the controlled lift in his voice that betrayed frustration.

'Hmmm, let me think,' said Unzen.

There was a long pause while Ryo waited for his answer. He was worried that he might have offended Unzen, that he might have overstepped the mark in asking such a question. After all, he was entirely dependent on his master for what he could teach him. Where else could he get any kind of training of this sort? He was just a potter's boy from a small village, with no special connections. What if Unzen sent him away for ingratitude? What would he do then? Where could he go but back home with his tail between his legs?

'Your training will begin very soon. The martial training, I mean. I have, though, been training you from day one, did you realize? But perhaps, since you bring it up, it's time to go a step further. Don't ask again. Just carry on as before. But tomorrow we'll begin when the time is right . . .'

Unzen left it at that and it was clear to Ryo that there was no more to be said about it. But he had an answer and it was a clear one. So that seemed promising. Tomorrow, his martial training . . . What would it consist of?

The next day began with no especial changes. His first task was to clip back the grass at the edge of the clearing. If it were left for too long it would grow back and gradually pull the settlement under the forest once again. Ryo had learned how nature reclaims all, if things are left untended for long enough. So he was clipping the grass and remembering the small garden area behind his parents' home. His work became automatic as his mind wandered back to thoughts of his family and his village.

All of a sudden there was a whack and he was sent sprawling headlong into the grass he'd been clipping. He was stunned, confused, his mind all of a whirl. The blow had come out of nowhere. Gathering his senses he turned with his arms raised to protect himself, lest another blow should land on him to follow the other. Unzen was standing above him with a long padded stick. The padding had protected Ryo from a serious wound, but all the same his shoulders were smarting from where the blow had landed. There would probably be a bruise and a dull ache to follow.

Ryo remonstrated with Unzen, so harsh had the blow seemed.

'Why did you strike me so hard? I am doing my duties. Did you guess my attention was wandering? Can you tell that by the way I'm working, by the way I'm doing things? Do you have the skill to mind-read? Was it a punishment for getting above myself last night? What should I think?'

Unzen simply spoke back kindly but firmly. 'No explanation. The next step of your training has begun. Be on your guard at all times. Continue with your duties . . .'

And with that he went back to whatever he was doing just out of Ryo's sight.

Why had Unzen done that? Was this some kind of punishment? It was true, his mind had been wandering. He had been instructed to perform tasks with full attention and not to daydream. Unzen used the word 'mindful' to describe this way of doing things. It meant focusing on the task in hand with full attention, not doing it in a dreamy way while thinking of other things. Unzen had said it was a way of preparing to be fully 'present' when facing an adversary. Ryo had grasped that this was one way in which 'learning to do ordinary things properly' might be his training already in progress.

From that time similar events took place. Whatever Ryo was doing, and somehow uncannily whenever his attention drifted, he would be attacked by Unzen, out of the blue with no warning. After the third of such attacks he realized that he had to be alert at all times if he was not to get hurt. He began to perform tasks using methods that allowed him to be sensitive to his surroundings as well as to what he was actually engaged with at the time. His senses were young and keen and he tuned them to be alert to sound and movement that might warn him of a surprise attack by Unzen. Soon he was whirling round even when a bird landed on a branch near his head or a mouse peeped out from the forest edge close to where he was working.

Gradually he grew better at discriminating between dangerous and safe sounds and movements. He even began to feel the very beginnings of a strange unnameable sense, more a feeling or presentiment of something about to happen. This was unreliable, as sometimes he turned swiftly yet found nothing there, and Unzen would be visible at the far side of the clearing, reading a scroll or mending a tool. He might just look up, catch Ryo's suspicious gaze and then nod, inscrutably. Sometimes Ryo had the sense of being teased. Was Unzen showing a sense of humour? It was hard to be sure and there would be no point in asking. If Unzen replied at all it would be with something that required a further question. Better for Ryo just to get on with his task and keep alert.

There was one occasion when he was scooping water into the wooden bucket. He was using a bamboo dipper to do this and was focused on the task in hand, as was expected of him. What alerted him he could not precisely say when thinking about it later. Had it been the light on the water darkening slightly? Was it the faintest rustle of clothing? Had he felt the faint vibration of a foot being placed behind him, nearby on the ground? Whatever it was he whirled round and hurled the water dipper at whatever was approaching. By now his reflexes were faster than his thoughts and this was sheer instinct working to protect him from a painful blow. As he took in what was happening he saw an arc of water from the dipper splashing over Unzen's body. Unzen caught the dipper neatly with one hand as it flew towards him.

Ryo gasped at his disrespect in giving Unzen, his master, a wetting. But Unzen was laughing. His weathered face seemed to crack open with mirth at the humour of what had happened.

'Oh, very good!' cried Unzen. 'And I could not avoid the water!'

Ryo, however, had not failed to notice how adroitly he had caught the dipper with no apparent effort. Yet again he was impressed at the skill and agility this old man could still call upon. He kept silent, however, and waited to hear if Unzen would say anything further.

'You've started to make your way through two important stages of training now. Neither are finished. In a way the stages are never finished. But once they are established in essence it's all right to proceed to the next stage. Gradually, the various stages begin to reinforce each other. You'll see how it is as we go on. That is, if you are sure you wish to go on. Tell me. Do you still wish to proceed? Are you still resolved?'

'Yes, indeed, master, I am still resolved,' said Ryo quickly, not wanting Unzen to be in any doubt about his determination.

'Well,' said Unzen, 'you've started to learn how to do things properly, with focused attention. And you've begun to learn to be alert to unexpected attacks at all times. Now we need to work on how to defend yourself efficiently when such attacks come at you, out of the blue, like that last one. There may not always be a water dipper to defend yourself with.'

He smiled as he said that and Ryo realized that he was joking. He was beginning to see that his master had a human side beneath the composed front he normally maintained. Unzen had warmth and humour that were not usually apparent.

'We'll start tomorrow. You'll begin to learn how to defend yourself from an attacker. In a way, that's more important than attacking and doing harm. How to avoid a blow, how to get out of the way of danger as it approaches. The art of not-fighting. The best kind of fighting there is.'

For a moment a memory flashed into Ryo's mind of Akio ducking from the brigand's sword swipe, Akio sidestepping his approach to catch him off balance, Akio using the brigand's own weight and force against the brigand himself. Yes, these were skills Ryo had come here to learn.

Chapter Seven

As Ryo's hand-to-hand training began it felt to him that at last he was doing what he had come for. For now he was starting to learn the skills he wanted to acquire. Yet he could already see the point of the preparatory stages that Unzen had put him through. He could grasp how attention to the precise way of doing things, along with full alertness and awareness of surrounding phenomena, would underpin any specific fighting skills one might develop for actual combat.

When it came to the training itself Unzen did not disappoint. It's true he was ageing and probably a shadow of his former self when a vigorous young man. But he was still way ahead of Ryo in both speed and strength. It seemed to Ryo almost magical how much Unzen could still do despite his age. He was well capable of challenging Ryo to bring forth his utmost.

'But you are still young,' Unzen said to Ryo in encouragement. 'We have started in good time. And you began with a good attitude. Your days in your father's workshop were put to good use. He passed on good principles to you. Working with clay was good preparation for working with air.'

Working with air. That was what Unzen sometimes called it. Or working with movement. Again, it made Ryo think of dancing, a sense of delicate agility and a kind of dancing around time and space and weight and force. Unzen said it was more like intervention than impact. Like intervening with the way things are, rather than pushing against them. For this art it was more useful to be sensitive, attentive, observant and swift, rather than heavy, powerful and weighty. Speed and dexterity would win over dogged brute force. This was how Akio had beaten the bandits.

From that time Ryo's training gathered speed. All kinds of specific learning took place: learning to duck and dodge, learning to get out of a tight corner, learning to avoid a blow while delivering one back in retaliation. Learning how to bring maximum force to a blow when absolutely necessary, yet how to reduce that force to minimize harm or damage to an opponent, if required.

There were days and days of one-to-one training sessions. Hours spent exercising, sometimes for strength, sometimes for flexibility, sometimes for balance and so forth. With such things to occupy them, along with the daily business of keeping the settlement in good order, time passed quickly. It was Unzen who pointed this out to Ryo at the end of another long day.

'It's been a while now since you first came here,' said Unzen to Ryo as they sipped tea by the fire early one evening. 'I kept a record of the day you arrived and my day-counter now shows me a full year. You've done well. You were right to come. Whatever happens from here, you have learned much.'

As Unzen spoke, Ryo found himself noting how much younger the old man seemed these days. Could it be that Unzen himself was getting something out of the training process? Perhaps it was not all one way. Maybe passing on his skills to a young learner had given him a new sense of purpose, something to liven up his life . . . ?

But Unzen was continuing to speak. 'There's not much more I can give you as a trainer of fighting. I'd need to be younger and fitter, especially since you're growing daily bigger and stronger. In fight skill I can teach you a little more, perhaps. But before I'm done there's something I can add to your repertoire while we're finishing the basic fight training.'

What could this be? wondered Ryo. Was there something more to be learned? Some different order of skill not touched on so far? He tried to imagine what it might be, but nothing would enter his mind to fill the space this question had opened up there. He waited to hear more, but Unzen had finished speaking. By now Ryo knew that all he had to do was wait. More would come when it was due.

'Most of what you've learned so far,' Unzen resumed the next day, 'has been about doing. It's been about fighting. About moving. About avoiding and delivering blows or pushes. But you'll notice that I've also been subtly training you how to "not-do" in amongst all the doing—'

'You mean when you've shown me how to wait, to see how an attacker comes at me?' Ryo cut in. It was unusual for him to interrupt while Unzen was instructing, but Unzen seemed unbothered.

He came straight back in, 'Yes, exactly so. It's the issue of stillness. About being absolutely in waiting-mode. Not passive. But alertly there, waiting for the first move so you can then respond appropriately.' Unzen grew quiet and thoughtful so that Ryo waited to hear what was coming next.

'That still state. You recall how we focused on the breathing as part of that stillness. You practised using the breath in order to be steady and ready. You remember how important I said it was to have good breath control in order to be at one with yourself. Also how it can be a good way to channel fear, to defuse feelings that make you less efficient in combat, less in control.'

Ryo nodded. He had absorbed those ideas well and

continued to practise them while training with Unzen.

'Well,' said Unzen, 'I want to show you more about stillness. About not-doing. In fact, about *being* rather than *doing*. There's a time to do, and a time to be. It's important to know the difference, and to know how just to *be* when there is nothing to be *doing*.'

Ryo was feeling a little light-headed with all this conceptual talk. It was beginning to sound like gobble-dygook, as they used to say back in Ryo's village.

As if in response to Ryo's state, Unzen cut himself off. 'But enough of all this theory. Better to show you. One action beats ten words with such things. I want you to learn how to *just-sit*. It may seem strange, but this is an ancient practice with much behind it. Better to do it than to speak of it, in order to learn from it.'

And so it was that Unzen began to teach Ryo about the art of quiet sitting. First they attended to the posture, how actually to sit in a way that enabled one to stay in position for a long time without getting stiff, sore, sleepy or wriggly. This maximized one's ability to remain alert while doing nothing. Once this was established Unzen told him about breathing, about breathing calmly and smoothly into the abdomen rather than the chest, about focusing attention on the breathing and about learning to acknowledge and then let go of the thoughts that were bound to arise in his mind while sitting in such a way, unoccupied.

Ryo learned to count breaths in a variety of ways, in order to maintain mental focus. And then to let go of the counting and simply follow the breath as it passed into and out of his body. Sometimes when practising this art he seemed to enter a kind of trance state, as if he was in some other dimension, as if, he fancied, he was sitting on the bed of the ocean and most of life was carrying on above him, above the surface of the sea.

When he told Unzen about this Unzen just smiled and said, 'Yes, these things happen. Don't set too much store by them. The mind, the body, the mind-body, it is a wonderful phenomenon, full of strangeness and mystery. But this is not magic, nor is it dreaming. It is just consciousness dancing its dance. Remember the posture . . . and the breathing. Those are the two key things to hold on to. Whatever else you may lose in your life, so long as you are still alive, you still have the posture . . . and the breathing. They will carry you through. Remember that, even if you don't understand it right now. Just remember it for the future. It may be the most important thing of all that I can teach you.' For a moment he looked deeply serious, thoughtful, reflective. Then he resumed. 'This has been about practice, about learning to practise a skill, this sitting and breathing and holding one's mind, one's being, in a kind of balance. There's a side to it I want to explore further with you, but not yet. Soon. When our minds are fresh and sharp. Tomorrow, maybe.'

Chapter Eight

'I want you to think,' said Unzen, 'about where you begin and where you end. Not in time, with birth and death, but in space. Consider. Can you answer the question, "What is you and what is not you?"'

Ryo thought about this. Was this a trick? Was there some catch in the question?

Unzen cut in, 'Don't think too hard. Just answer in any way that seems obvious.'

Ryo patted himself with his hands. His head, his chest, his hips, his legs. 'This is me.' And then he patted at the air around himself, as if pushing it away. 'And this is not me.' He smiled towards Unzen in a puzzled way, curious. Then he thought, and quickly added, 'My skin, and what's inside it, is me. What's beyond my skin and outside of it, apart from my hair and my nails, is not me. *Me* is contained by my skin, I think.'

'So it would seem,' said Unzen. 'But answer me. Is there anything out there, beyond your skin, that enters you at any time?'

Ryo thought further. Then he added brightly, 'Well, food, of course. Oh, and drink. What I eat and drink enter me, pass through me, and come out at the other end. Though some of it becomes me, I think. It feeds my growing.'

'So you are admitting that you do not really have an existence independent from the rest of the world, by saying that? Although you can move about upon the surface of the world you do not really have a separate existence . . . ?' Before Ryo could answer this Unzen was pressing him further. 'But is there something else you may be forgetting, some other part or parts of the world that may be within you, even though they appear to be without you, outside of you?'

Ryo looked puzzled.

Suddenly Unzen spoke to him in training tone. 'Quick, hold your breath! Sit still and hold your breath. Shut your mouth and pinch your nose tightly.'

Ryo did so.

'Now stay like that.'

Ryo was used to following instructions when Unzen spoke in this way. There was always a point being made. Unzen never asked Ryo to do anything for no reason. So he just did so. After a while he began to grow sick and dizzy until at last he gasped for air and stood breathing deeply and shaking his head gently from side to side.

'Air,' he said, 'air . . .'

'Quite so,' said Unzen. 'You are not separate from the world around you. You have the sense of being a separate, independent being. But in truth you are connected to all that surrounds you, near or far. Look at that tree there.' He pointed to the cherry tree at the edge of the clearing. 'Now shut your eyes. Can you see the tree in your mind's eye?'

'Yes,' said Ryo. He opened his eyes to see the tree more clearly. Then he shut them again. 'Yes, even better now.'

'So tell me,' pressed Unzen. 'Is the tree out there or in here?' He tapped at Ryo's head with his forefinger.

Ryo thought very hard for a moment. 'Well, kind of both, I think,' he said slowly. 'I mean, it would not appear to be there to me . . . if I were not here to see it, I think . . .' He pointed over to the tree and back to his own eyes and then moved his fingers back and forth, pointing first at the tree, then back at his own eyes.

'So you see,' said Unzen, 'that perhaps life is more about relationships than about separate things? Existence can seem to be about real solid things. But where will the cherry tree be a thousand years from now? And where will you be then?'

'Neither of us will be at all,' said Ryo. 'We will both

have passed on, as all things do, as I've always been told. As my father showed me when my pet mouse died when I was little. I know that all living things die sooner or later and that most things in the end rot away, turn to dust or are burned to ashes. But I cannot see what this has to do with fighting. I can't see why we are talking of these things . . .'

'It's a question of how deeply you want to do things. A question of how intense your engagement is with what you do. I know your father is a potter. Does he just make rough pots and cups for villagers or does he make fine things, beautiful things, things that have *presence*?' Unzen paused before the word 'presence' and spoke it with a kind of special emphasis.

Ryo answered him. 'Well, he does make ordinary things for villagers, things they use in their daily lives. But even then they are well made and have a kind of simple beauty of their own. And he used to say to me in the workshop, "Only make what is useful or beautiful. If possible, both." And sometimes he makes vases for flower arrangements, or tea bowls for tea ceremony. He takes great care with such work. As much care as you teach me to do things here, I would say.'

'Well, I am saying to you now, Ryo, that fighting can be carried out with as much reverence and care as making fine pots, as your father clearly does. So if you go on to be a true fighter, a fine fighter, a deep fighter, you will not have come so very far from your father's workshop after all. It will not be so very different than if you had stayed with him and learned the deep art of pottery. Are you sure you shouldn't return home now to pursue that course? Are you sure you are following the best way, here with me? Don't answer. I just want you to hold that question in your mind and in your heart, in your heart-mind, and let it dwell there. An answer will arise for you in due course. Neither you nor I can force it. Let it be for now. Just remember it from time to time so the question stays alive.'

Unzen paused for a moment and looked thoughtful. 'I want to tell you a story. Now would be a good time. These things we speak of are deep and difficult things for someone of your age, and at your stage. Sometimes a story strikes deeper and truer than mere ideas. Listen and I'll tell it.

'There was once a farmer who accidentally bumped into a swordsman in such a way as to cause offence. The swordsman quickly challenged him to a duel, and back in those times once such a challenge was made it could not be withdrawn. The farmer could not refuse. Custom demanded he show up for the fight. In despair he went to visit a trainer of sword-combat to see if he could learn anything about sword technique that might help him.

'"Forget it," said the teacher. "You must simply accept that you are going to die. In a week I can teach you just one stance and one cut. If you master these you may at least stand a chance of delivering one blow back as you die. At least you will salvage some honour that way."

'The farmer spent the week coming to terms with the prospect of dying, as if he were going to his execution. He sat contemplating death, while breathing and staying focused. He also practised his one stance, holding a sword correctly, and his one cut, learning to deliver the stroke exactly as the sword-trainer had shown him. By the appointed time of the duel he could hold his sword, his stance and his readiness for death in a steady and determined way.

'He took up his position as the swordsman approached. He managed to hold his concentration. He was looking death straight in the face without flinching. He had completely accepted the fact of his imminent death and simply held his stance. When the swordsman made his move he would deliver back his one practised blow. At least then honour would be maintained, and in those days honour stood above all else, even above life itself.

'The swordsman started to weave around in front of him, making feints to provoke him to make his move. But he would not be goaded. He knew to wait till the swordsman made a real attack before delivering his blow. He just went on standing, facing death and holding his sword raised in the correct way.

'Eventually the swordsman sighed and stepped back. "Amazing," he said with admiration. "You may be a farmer but you have the heart and spirit of a true warrior. I cannot break your defence. I could kill you but I would myself be killed by your prepared blow as I did so. Foolish for us both to die. I withdraw my challenge. The fight ends with a draw. As challenger I am permitted to do that. Our quarrel is over." And off he went, leaving the farmer to adjust to the fact that he was in fact going to live on after all.'

Ryo sat musing on the details of the story. Unzen had told it with vivid simplicity. The farmer's plight had lodged in Ryo's mind. He imagined himself in that situation. To have to look death in the face and wait for it to happen, without flinching or breaking down. Could he, Ryo, ever do that?

'Let me spell it out,' Unzen resumed after a pause. 'I tell you that story purely to describe the farmer's attitude to his own death, his relation to it. As a fighter, if you intend to become a deep and true fighter, like your hero Akio, then you have to cultivate a state of being without fear.

'You are fighting not to protect yourself, or others, or what you own or believe in. You may be doing all those things, of course, and I wish you only ever to fight for good and just causes. But *when* you fight, *if* you fight, when the actual business of fighting occurs, then it is essential in my view to be entirely committed to the fighting in the same way your father is committed to the clay when he is making a precious vase. Fighting may be a way of protecting and preserving in the same way that pots and cups are a means of eating and drinking and storing things. But in itself fighting can be an art and even a *way*.' He said 'way' with that special emphasis that Ryo had heard his father say it, when talking seriously about the art of pottery as a way of life.

And gradually Ryo's young mind was beginning to grasp the essence of such instruction from Unzen. From time to time it seemed to make sense, a kind of felt-sense, to Ryo. He could not have expressed it in words. He could not have explained to me or you how it worked. But it was as if Unzen's teaching was beginning to seep into him, as if he was starting to soak it up. And then it would slip away again and he would be baffled by what Unzen was telling him.

But through all this Unzen would say, 'Don't try to get it with your mind. It's not school learning. Just remember the main words and hold them. Let your deep understanding work on them by itself. Absorb the ideas and allow your being to let them "take". Think of them as seeds planted in the soil of your being. Allow them time to grow as nature does a plant. It will all come with time . . .'

CHAPTER NINE

It was not long after that serious conversation between them that Unzen broached the subject of Ryo's future with him. They had just finished their evening meal and were sitting on the rough wooden stools, warming themselves by the glowing embers of the fire. As usual they were sipping tea from the small, clay bowls that Unzen always poured the steaming liquid into.

'I think it's time for you to move on now,' said Unzen in that even way he had of delivering news or information.

For a moment Ryo froze. Was he being sent on his way? Was this the end of his training with Unzen? Where would he go? What would he do? He hadn't planned beyond this. This news was so sudden. He hadn't even begun to consider where he might go once Unzen had taught him all he could.

Unzen caught sight of his startled expression and smiled. 'Don't worry, there's a clear path to follow. I am not abandoning you. You will not be thrown out into the world without support or guidance. I am simply telling you that at this stage you need to pass on to training that I can no longer supply at my age and with the limitations of our small settlement here.'

Ryo noticed he said 'our' as if Ryo really belonged there and was part of the Cold Mountain Hermitage, as Unzen sometimes now playfully called it. It warmed him to think of this place as a kind of second home, with Unzen as a dignified yet kindly uncle. He had had no contact with his real home or family since he'd come to Cold Mountain and his sense of belonging was now focused on this little camp where he spent all his days.

'A short time from now,' Unzen resumed, 'I'll be taking you to the Hill Camp of the Hidden Ones. I've refrained from speaking of them to you up till now. This is because I wanted you to be entirely focused on what you were doing here with me. I did not want you to be distracted by thoughts and ideas of a future else-where. I did not want your mind to be on a further objective. But it's time for you to be going on from me, as I just said. So I'm telling you now that in a few days' time we'll be travelling further into the mountains to the Hill Camp where you'll be staying for your training with the Hidden Ones. I'll be your guide. It's almost impossible to find the place unless you know the way. They're not called "the Hidden Ones" for nothing,' he smiled.

Ryo's unease had shifted to excitement and apprehension at the mention of the Hidden Ones. He knew exactly where he'd heard that phrase before. It was firmly imprinted on his memory. He could still visualize Akio, his hero, saying the words to the brigands back in his village on that day when Ryo's life had changed. He could still remember the sense of mystery, thrill and fascination it had kindled in him.

Anticipating further questions from Ryo, Unzen continued. 'I will not be staying long there with you. Once I have introduced you I will return here after a short rest. After that I can't say when we will next meet. Perhaps never . . .' He paused, as if reflecting on this, and for a moment Ryo thought he saw a flicker of sadness cross the old man's face. But then it was gone and Unzen was talking once more in his dignified, slightly formal style.

'You will learn much there that I cannot teach you here, for the camp, if it is still as I last saw it, is full of youngsters such as yourself. And it is run by many mature, fully fledged artists. Artists such as Akio, who protected your village.'

Ryo pricked up his ears to hear them described as 'artists' rather than 'warriors' or 'fighters'. As always, listening carefully to Unzen when he spoke gave one new things to consider, new ways to perceive and understand the world and one's life in it.

Over the following days Ryo continued to live and train with Unzen, as before. They maintained the regime of work, exercise, combat training, quiet sitting and conversation. There was one important exchange that took place the evening before they left for the inner mountains. It was a kind of gathering up of things that had been talked about and practised during Ryo's training. This was a conversation Ryo never forgot.

'I'm going to say some things to you now that I want you to listen to carefully,' Unzen began. He paused, waiting to see that Ryo was fully focused on him, then resumed. 'You've spent over a year now just with me. We've been alone here together and the only other person you've seen, and briefly at that, has been the Bringer, the man who brings our basic supplies. Word has gone back with him, by the way, to let your family know that you are in good health and working hard. I did not mention this to you as I did not want you to attempt to send them messages of any kind. I did not want you distracted from your purposes by such considerations. But I wanted them to be reassured of your welfare. I knew they would be thinking of you, missing you and concerned about your wellbeing.'

Ryo felt a rush of feeling and longing for his family.

At their mention he envisaged them there in the little hut in the village, as ever, as he'd left them. He often thought of them, of course, but he had learned to put the thought aside and not to long to see them. He had made a choice, which meant being away from home for perhaps a long time. In due course, maybe, he'd be in a position to write them a letter and have it delivered. But for now he just thought of them briefly each day and sent his love across the sky to them as a kind of imaginary prayer. He thought of them doing the same back to him. And it comforted him. But Unzen was continuing to speak.

'So I want you to be clear in your mind, before you go on to the next stage of training, that your family have been assured of your wellbeing and that they, in turn, from what I've been told, are much as you left them.' He cleared his throat. 'But there's another matter I want to speak about. As I was saying, you've been alone here with me on Cold Mountain. At the Hill Camp you'll be surrounded by others. And you'll all be training hard together and living closely. What I have to say concerns your relation to yourself and in turn to others. Some of it we will have spoken of before. This is a kind of putting together of the fuller picture, I might say.'

Unzen paused again, as if gathering up his thoughts before proceeding to a further level. 'It could be said that your experience is made up of three main elements: mental events, physical events and emotions. While it's possible to define them as separate categories, often they come tangled together. For instance an embarrassing thought, like the thought of being in public with no clothes on, while it's a thought it also comes with an emotion and also with a physical sensation: the emotion is one of feeling flustered, anxious and uncomfortable and the physical sensation might be a hotness in the cheeks, a blushing and a shortness of breath. But, in short, most of our experience is a kind of mixture of mental thought, emotional feeling and physical sensation. Are you still with me?' Unzen looked directly at Ryo who was concentrating hard.

He nodded, 'Yes, I think I understand that, yes.'

Unzen resumed. 'Have you ever noticed, when sitting, when doing our quiet sitting, our "just sitting", that there can at times be a part of you that is a kind of "watcher within", a quiet observer that can detach, separate itself from internal events and watch them as they take place? As if you become the viewer of your own experience? As if you can observe your thoughts and feelings and sensations arising and passing on while that silent observer in you just watches . . . ?'

'Yes!' Ryo exclaimed suddenly, forgetting manners and etiquette for a moment.

Unzen smiled at his youthful energy. 'Ah, I see I

have hooked you now. You are with me. Tell me more.'

'Well,' said Ryo, pausing for a moment to clarify his mind. 'It's when we do sitting quietly and follow-the-breath exercise. So often when we do that my mind keeps coming up with all sorts of things. I know that when that happens I'm meant to just note it and then let it go and return to focusing on my breathing, the in . . . and the out . . . but sometimes strong feelings come, like when thoughts of my family come into my mind . . . and sometimes I get a pain in my legs or shoulders, or anywhere, just from sitting still for so long. And when all that is happening I'm sometimes aware that there's this bit of me that is watching everything else. Not doing anything to it or with it, but just quietly seeing it all as it is. I've started to call it my "Deep Me", my "Hidden Me". It's almost like the inmost bit of me.'

'Now,' said Unzen, taking up the reins again, 'you will be needing that part of you in the months to come. In fact, throughout the rest of your life, if you are to lead it with full attention. That part of you will help you to make one of the most important choices there is . . .' He saw Ryo frown and hastened to address the question he had prompted. 'Don't worry. I will explain. I'm getting there. The choice I'm talking about is one we make many times a day. It's not a single, one-time choice. It's a choice which crops up over and over. It's the choice of whether to react or respond.'

Now Ryo really *was* puzzled. He had not encountered this distinction before.

Unzen could read the uncertainty on his face so he proceeded with great care. 'Whenever someone says or does something to you that requires you to speak or act, the standard thing is to speak or act in reaction to what has been said or done. For the untrained person this is instinctive, automatic, we might say. Depending on our own particular character we each behave in a way that, for us, is almost reflex. Anyone who knows us well can often predict what we will do or say. It could be said to be our "character" or our "nature". More accurately, I think, it's probably our "habit", our set of beliefs and principles built up, without thought or planning, from our past experience.'

Ryo was listening, so Unzen persisted. 'The trouble with *reaction*,' he stressed the word, 'is that it very often makes things worse, puts more fuel on the flames, so to speak. Someone snaps at you. You snap back. And soon you are quarrelling or even fighting. And neither person is truly listening to what the other is saying. What one is trying to say gets wrapped around with the other's personal clouds of concern. Or if someone does something that offends or annoys you, you feel you have to intervene and complain or object or kick back at them in some way. And, again, it just makes things worse and doesn't undo the original misdeed, as you see it.

'The *skilful* thing to do' – every so often Unzen would pause and put a heavy emphasis on a word, as if underlining it in speech) – 'is not to react, but to *respond.*'

'I don't see the difference,' protested Ryo. 'Surely they mean the same thing, those two words . . . ?'

'Ah, but I am making a distinction,' smiled Unzen. 'I am using "react" to describe what we do when we behave automatically, without thinking. I'm using "respond" for when we put that hidden, inner self in control. The inner self pauses and holds back from instant action. It separates itself from the moment just enough to give time to consider what best to say or do, rather than doing what comes "naturally". Sometimes it can result in not-saying or not-doing at all. The main thing is that it allows time to read the situation more fully before ploughing in with words and actions that may be unhelpful, or that may make things worse.'

Ryo nodded. 'Yes, I think I see the difference there . . .'

'This can be most useful when in company, with others, as you will be at the Hill Camp. It's a helpful thing to have ready when interacting with others. But it's also part of the art of fighting.' Unzen dropped that last remark in suddenly, surprising Ryo with this seeming change of subject. He registered the look of confusion entering Ryo's face.

'Ah, it's not so strange when you think of it,' Unzen was quick to resume. 'It's true that reflex can be important for sudden moves, at times. When the water ladle hurtles at your head,' he smiled as he said this, 'your hand catches it automatically without your mind deciding. It just happens naturally. But what you do next should be a matter of response not reaction, if you are a truly trained artist. So having this slight detachment there can prompt you to size up the situation before barging in where you're not required or where your interference will make matters worse.' Unzen paused briefly, took a breath and smiled at Ryo. 'What I am saying to you now is the inmost, most essential part of your training in the art of fighting. No matter how skilful, strong, fit, swift, nimble, alert and so forth you become, all of this will be as nothing if you do not nurture in yourself this essential skill I have just described.'

Unzen saw doubt flicker across Ryo's face. 'I can see you resist what I am saying and I can understand your difficulty with it. You want to be a great fighter like Akio. You want to do good with it. You want to bring greater justice and peace to the world by protecting others. These are all very worthy sentiments. But I tell you now that they will be misused, or at least always prone to misuse, if you do not cultivate in yourself this skill of detachment. If your prowess in fighting is the body, then this skill is the breath. Without the breath the body is simply useless baggage. It's that important. It doesn't matter if you don't understand right now. You don't have to say you believe me this very moment. Simply remember what I've said. Store it in your memory. Experience will show you whether it is true or not. Remember the words. Leave life to do the testing out for you.'

If Ryo still felt any doubts about what he had been hearing they were swept away by what he saw next.

Unzen stood up swiftly and assumed a fighting pose. 'And as for fighting,' he said, moving gracefully as if confronting an adversary, 'some of what you learn will become reflex, necessarily. No use in delaying response when a blow is coming down on you, or an arrow flying through the air or two attackers running from different directions. Some skills, especially defensive ones, need to be always present, as if on your skin itself, ready to protect you so you can then act decisively as required . . .' He went into a swift series of moves as if avoiding blows, dodging weapons and delivering pushes, kicks and punches all at great speed and with the fluency of a well-practised dance.

Ryo gasped at how this old man could still do such things. As he did so he remembered Akio and the brigands, back in his village. Whenever he saw Unzen in action like this it reminded him of Akio, as if Akio was in some way Unzen as a younger man. Was it the style of the movements? Could Unzen once have been Akio's teacher? Had Akio learned his skills from Unzen, as he, Ryo, was doing now?

It seemed possible, likely even. Perhaps when the moment felt right he would ask Unzen.

CHAPTER TEN

It was only two days later that Unzen and Ryo set out for the Hill Camp. The day before had been spent tidying up their own small camp, leaving things in good order against Unzen's return, preparing food for the journey, leaving the vegetable patch well watered and likely to survive Unzen's absence. And making their travel bundles conveniently portable so they could walk unhampered.

They had been sitting by the fire the night before leaving when Ryo had asked quietly, 'Master Unzen, were you once Akio's teacher? Did he learn from you?'

As usual, Unzen paused before replying. Then, 'Yes,' he said simply. 'He was once my pupil . . .' He stopped there but looked thoughtful, as if remembering times past. 'He was a good pupil, the best ever, I think.

Though one can never be sure at the time what life will bring to people and how they might develop. He became a great fighter, a true artist, though he could still develop further if he persisted.'

Ryo hesitated, then ventured, 'Master, am I a good pupil? Do I have it in me to become a great fi— I mean . . . a great artist? Could I be like Akio?'

Unzen smiled at him and looked into his eyes with unusual warmth. 'Ryo, you will never be like Akio. Akio is Akio and Ryo is Ryo. You each have your own centre and your own being. I'm not sure you could ever be as effective a fighter as Akio. But I am not the ultimate judge and people can surprise us. They can even surprise themselves. You have something special that Akio had less of back then. This is why sometimes I've questioned your desire to learn the art of fighting from me. Fighting is at best defensive, at worst destructive. From you so often I get the sense of someone creative. The fact that your father is a potter could account for that. If it were for me to choose your life I would have you be a potter . . . or a painter . . . or a poet. But it's for you to choose your life and you seem to choose the way of fighting. There is much to be learned from that way and some of the best of it lies not in the fighting itself but in the inner qualities of the art. And those will serve you well whatever way your future life goes.'

Exasperated, Ryo persisted, as if Unzen had not spoken, 'But tell me, please, master, is it possible that I might, just might, match up to Akio in terms of fighting skill . . . ?' He looked so desperate for a moment that Unzen let out a kindly laugh. It was rare to hear him laugh.

'Oh, Ryo, yes! Perhaps one day you will be the greatest fighter the world has ever seen and you will eventually have defeated all potential rivals and enemies. You will stand on the pinnacle of success, just as a person may stand at the top of the highest mountain. But tell me – what will you do then? What will come next?' He saw Ryo looking puzzled, not knowing whether he was being teased or seriously instructed, so he changed his tone and spoke more plainly. 'Remember what you've learned from me. Not to dwell too much on the past, worrying about whether you've misused your time up to now. For there is nothing you can do to change that. And not to fret about the future, becoming anxious about whether you'll ever achieve what you think you're aiming for right now. But to focus mostly on the present, doing properly, as best you can, the thing that has to be done at this moment, this present but fluent moment. How does one eat a mountain of rice? A few bowls per day. How does one travel a thousand miles? A few miles a day, one step at a time. How does one read a library of books and scrolls? One sentence at a time. Word by word, bit by bit. How does a snail climb Mount Fuji? Inch by inch, with present attention. And with patience.'

Unzen gathered himself as his speech ended. 'But now, my friend, it is time we slept. We need to start the day tomorrow well rested. Tomorrow we walk. Tonight we sleep. Breath by breath.' And he winked at Ryo and grinned, which was a most unusual thing for him to do. Perhaps he was letting go of being Ryo's master? Perhaps he was relaxing and preparing to pass Ryo on to his future teachers.

And that night, his last night in the camp, Ryo dreamed. In his dream he was back in his father's workshop. He was sitting at the wheel, bringing a beautiful pot into being out of an inert lump of clay. The vase rose radiantly, with elegant grace and poise. It seemed to quiver there, already emanating a kind of power even in its raw clay state. What a fine vase it would be once glazed and fired! And then suddenly the head brigand had clattered into the workshop in his clumsy war gear and was raising his sword to swipe at Ryo's pot. Ryo put out his hands to protect the pot and the sword sliced through them, cutting them off at the wrist before also cleaving the pot into two neat halves, so sharp was the blade. Ryo woke startled from his dream, the vision still clear in his head. Such a thing must never happen. If he learned to be like Akio he could prevent it. He must realize his aim of becoming a great fighter.

But now they were setting out. Unzen paused at the edge of their settlement as Ryo waited for him.

'Come, Ryo, look,' murmured Unzen.

Ryo approached and stood near him.

Unzen spoke less formally than was usual. 'This is where it began for you. You could say that it began back in your village when you saw Akio challenge the brigands. You could even go further back than that, perhaps. But this is where your formal training began. This is where you planted the seed and let it take root. Don't forget it. It is, it was, an important stage in your progress.'

Unzen then made a deep *gassho*, the bow of respect and courtesy towards someone or something that respect was due to. Seeing this, Ryo did the same. It seemed a little strange to bow to the settlement, but he understood what Unzen meant.

And then they set off. They did not go back the way Ryo had first come to Cold Mountain. They left Cold Mountain Hermitage by the upper way out. Ryo had never been that way before. Unzen had not allowed it. When he'd had time to rest and be alone he'd been permitted to go down the path to where there were one or two views back over the way he had first travelled to Cold Mountain. But Unzen had told him that the upper path was reserved for a time when Ryo might be 'ready for it'. Ryo had never exactly known what that meant, but he'd been forced to accept it. And now the mystery was over. He was 'ready' to pass on and up and he would see what lay ahead, quite literally.

What lay ahead at times took his breath away. Ryo had never quite fully realized how vast the world was. The upper path went up and up. At one point there was a dividing of the ways, a fork.

Unzen pointed to the left way. 'That is the way to the top of Cold Mountain,' he told Ryo. 'It is rare for anyone ever to go there. They say the Wind Dragons, the cloud blowers, nest there. If ever you come to seek me and cannot find me at the Hermitage, go up there and look. I may be there. But our way now is this.' He pointed to the right path, which ran lower and curved around the mountain.

As they followed this lower path they soon came to a large boulder that lay across the narrow track. It was split down the middle, creating just a wide enough gap for a person with their pack to get through. Unzen directed Ryo to go through first. As he came out of the narrow fissure he gasped. The range of mountains seemed to go on for ever, as if rolling into eternity, into infinity, into the great beyond that the poets spoke of. Where, in all that mass of mountains, might the Hill Camp be? How could anyone ever find it without a map?

And yet Unzen seemed to have no trouble. Whenever they came to a dividing of the ways, or a part of the journey where no path was evident, Unzen paused, closed his eyes, then nodded and went on decisively. There was clearly some method for remembering the way, unless Unzen had walked it so often he was able to recall it. Now and then they came to a stream to cross, or running close to the path. Whenever this occurred Unzen called a halt and they would drink from the stream, wash their faces and their feet and refill their water vessels. Sometimes they paused to rest, occasionally taking something to eat, one of the rice balls they had prepared, or some dried mushroom or salted plum, for instance.

'Will we get there today?' Ryo asked politely during one of these breaks.

'Tomorrow,' Unzen replied. 'About midday tomorrow. If it were urgent we could make it by tonight. But it would be best to arrive fresh and rested. So we will stop overnight not so very far from the camp itself. A short morning's walk, let us say.'

After that Ryo found he could relax more into the journey, allowing his curiosity and anticipation to settle into the next day, leaving him free to be more in each moment, as Unzen so often advised he should try to be.

They passed no one on their journey. Eventually

Ryo questioned Unzen about this. 'Does nobody live here?' he asked. 'Are there no villages or farms hereabout?'

Unzen smiled and shook his head. 'It's too inhospitable. The effort of settling up here is too great for most people. Some of the villages nearest to this refer to it as the Great Vast or the Great Waste. It's reckoned that only some animals survive here and maybe a few brigands, though I think that most brigands would find it a challenge to live here. Besides, the Hidden Ones would soon see them off.'

'So how do the Hidden Ones survive here?' pressed Ryo.

'Oh, you'll see how that works tomorrow,' said Unzen. 'Wait until you can see it for yourself.'

When evening came they stopped beside a stream where a few trees grew. It seemed a perfect place to camp for the night.

Unzen sniffed the air. 'No need for a shelter,' he said. 'There'll be no rain. No need for a fire, either. The air is warm and there are no wild beasts to ward off. And better not to leave signs of human presence too near to the Hill Camp. Better to leave no trace when we go. Leave it as we find it. The best way, whenever possible.'

Ryo listened to Unzen's voice. He had become accustomed to Unzen thinking aloud like this. It was part of his training method. By thinking aloud he would pass on ways of thinking, reasons for action or non-action, a whole way of behaving and being. It was clear to Ryo that Unzen intended him gradually to soak up these things by being with him. This was learning from life not just from words. Ryo thought he would miss it once they had parted.

They sat quietly for a while, resting from the journey and going into themselves, the way Unzen had taught him to do. Then Unzen roused and they fetched water from the stream and drank it with a few of their provisions. It was a simple, quiet, thoughtful supper. Before they retired to sleep Unzen said just a few more things to Ryo.

'When we arrive at the Hill Camp I will take you to meet the Elders. Then they will assign you to a group, most probably. That will be a group of young ones such as yourself, in training. I will stay to talk some more with the Elders and then come to say goodbye to you. After that I may not see you for a long time. Perhaps never. But whatever, our time together at Cold Mountain is over. It has served its purpose and you must now press on with your intentions. Let's sleep now. Get some good rest and prepare for your new life tomorrow.'

They unrolled their blankets and found places near to one another where the grass was soft. Putting their bundles by their heads and settling into their blankets, they fell silent and still. Unzen seemed to fall asleep almost instantly, but Ryo lay on his back for a while, gazing up between the trees at the deepening night sky above him. The stars had begun to show and he found himself becoming aware of the vastness of the heavens, which now seemed to match the wideness of the Great Waste that he was travelling through. He felt suddenly very small, very tiny, ant-like in proportion to the hugeness of it all. And being weary from his day's walking, he too was soon asleep.

The next day they rose early. Ryo felt refreshed after a good sleep on the soft grass, warm in his blanket. The night had been mild. They washed in the stream, took a brief breakfast, fastened up their bedding and bundles and were away early along the track. They had said little, almost nothing, while rising. And they walked quietly too, not chatting, but simply going along while Ryo took in his surroundings as they gradually changed.

Towards the middle of the morning Ryo began to make out a rise in the distance. It was like a huge hill with no top, like a sugarloaf with the crest cut off. It reminded him in shape of the images of Mount Fuji, the sleeping volcano, that his father sometimes painted on the side of pots. Only this was lower, more squat, less like a mountain and more like a climbable hill. As they grew closer Ryo could make out a path leading up it. Could this be the Hill Camp at last?

'Is that where we're going?' asked Ryo.

'Yes,' Unzen replied. But he said nothing more and just kept walking.

Ryo followed him in silence.

The way up the hill was not easy. It was steep in parts and by the time they reached the crest Ryo felt spent. Anyone intending to attack this place would be exhausted by the time they arrived here. Defenders at the top would have immediate advantage. This was clearly no coincidence. This was planned.

As they came to the rim of what was clearly now a crater two young men appeared as if from nowhere. For a moment they looked challenging, as if to bar the visitors from entering. But as their gazes fell on Unzen their manner changed utterly. Their faces took on looks of respect and they both bowed, the full deep bow reserved for greeting someone of high status.

'Sensei,' they both said, almost in chorus.

'Sensei' was the word for 'master' or 'teacher' or 'leader'. Ryo sometimes used that word when addressing Unzen, especially when receiving formal instruction. Did Unzen have special status here? Ryo felt suddenly abashed to be in the company of someone important. Was there more to Unzen than he had assumed? After all, he had never heard Unzen's story.

The two young men were clearly on some kind of lookout duty. From the rim you could see for miles. The rim was wide, circling what Ryo now saw was a large area within, shallowly set into the top of the hill. There were fields at the far side where crops were growing and others where animals grazed, goats, it looked like from here. But down in the centre of the natural basin was a large camp, a village, even, by its size and the nature of the huts. There was a hall which seemed the most important building, and a few more slightly smaller halls. And then many huts that looked like living accommodation. Everywhere Ryo looked he could see people moving about. And then he spotted an area where figures were exercising, and another area where couples and groups were engaged in what looked like combat. But every now and then they stopped and seemed to be talking before resuming. He saw one or two moves that he recognized. Those were moves he had learned from Unzen. He knew how to parry those himself. For a moment he felt pleased and proud. Then he saw two figures engaged with each other. He was amazed by what they could do with their bodies. The speed, the balance, the poise, the subtlety. He realized on seeing that that he had much still to learn.

As Ryo stood looking at all this Unzen waited patiently. He knew this sight would have an impact on Ryo and he wanted it to take effect on him. If the boy was to train here he needed to have a good sense of what he was taking on. If this was to be his new home he wanted Ryo to have a clear picture of it from outside, before getting involved in the busy thick of it.

Ryo sensed Unzen waiting patiently and shook himself out of his absorption. 'Forgive me, master. I am keeping you waiting.'

'It's all right,' said Unzen informally. 'This is the Hill Camp. You are here at last. Pause here and take it in before we go and make our greetings. Today there is no hurry. Let's do this properly. Step by step.'

Ryo looked a little longer, but once he had the general impression of things he began to want to go down and see them at close quarters. He looked at Unzen and said quietly, 'I'm ready now. Shall I follow you down?'

Unzen led the way as if very familiar with it. They passed some younger people, both boys and girls, mostly Ryo's own age, or thereabouts. The young folk looked at Unzen curiously and whispered to one another. As Unzen and Ryo passed them the youngsters gave them a formal greeting and it was clear they had no idea who Unzen was. But when they approached a group of young men, Unzen again received what seemed to Ryo like real veneration. These men held Unzen in high esteem. They knew who he was and must have known him already to be so sure of his status.

'Master, are you known here?' whispered Ryo quizzically.

'I would say so. I used to run the place. I established it. I set it up many years ago. But I stood down some time back now. I appointed a successor and retired to Cold Mountain. But I try to visit once in a while. Bringing you here has given me an opportunity to see how the old place is looking. They're not doing badly. They have many recruits. And some of them are girls. That's important. They bring balance. The presence of the feminine keeps the masculine steady. Without that the boys go a little crazy. Yang and Yin, as they say.'

They continued to walk through the settlement. As they went along many of the older members bowed and greeted Unzen, some with apparent warmth and pleasure, some with more awe and respect. Unzen responded to all with an easy manner as if he felt very much at home here.

Eventually they came to the great hall, the largest of the buildings. As they approached a figure stepped out to receive them. News had somehow gone ahead of them that visitors were arriving and this person was ready to receive them formally. The figure was already in a deep bow as they reached the steps. When he rose Ryo looked at him and his mouth fell open. For a moment he forgot his manners and just gaped. It was

Akio. Seeing Ryo in such a state, Akio merely raised an eyebrow and looked to Unzen.

'Sensei,' he said with a voice full of warmth and feeling, while his body betrayed no emotion.

'Akio,' Unzen replied, bowing back.

Then the formality was over and both men relaxed into friendly chat, for a moment ignoring Ryo completely. He stood there in the presence of these established men, feeling like a youngster, an apprentice, a servant boy. How had he deserved such special treatment so far? What could they possibly think he might have to offer? For a moment he felt like a fraud, an impostor. How had he presumed to go to Cold Mountain? How had he imagined that Unzen would think him worth taking on?

But now Unzen was turning to him to introduce him properly to Akio.

'Akio, this is Ryo. Ryo, this is Akio.' Unzen spoke the words formally in a loud, clear voice, obviously intending all around to hear him. Then he dropped his voice and spoke less formally, 'I believe you may have met before?' He spoke that last question more like a statement, and with a twinkle in his eye.

Ryo paused, waiting to hear what would be said or done next. Akio took the initiative. He made another bow and looked into Ryo's face as he spoke.

'Welcome to the Hill Camp. You have been very

determined to get here. So now I welcome you to our company and invite you to become one of us. Do you accept?'

'Yes,' Ryo said quietly but clearly. He gave a formal bow to confirm his reply.

Akio bowed back. 'Yokoso!' he called in a loud voice, using the word for 'welcome'.

Then all who were within earshot echoed him in unison to create a combined shout, 'YOKOSO!'

And then the word was taken up across the camp by all who had heard it, so that as it was heard further and further away it was echoed again and again until it had rippled out to the farthest extremity, as if a pebble had been dropped into a pond to create ripples that eddied outward to the far edges.

Ryo flushed to hear himself so firmly accepted by all. For a moment he wondered whether he could live up to being a part of such a company. But now Akio was talking to him again.

'It's already clear that you wish to join us and learn our ways. Unzen would not have brought you here had he not been sure about that himself. The fact you are here is proof of your commitment so far. In a moment you will have a little time to say farewell to your teacher and then you will be taken to the group you are to lodge with. They will be your companions while you stay and train as a junior. They will explain all you need to know about how we do things here. Think of them, in a way, as your family at the Hill Camp. You'll come to know them well.'

Akio turned to the small crowd that had gathered around to witness Ryo's acceptance. 'Dokemasu!' he said simply, giving the signal for them to return to their duties. Then he turned back to Ryo and said gently, 'Take a little time to say your goodbyes to Unzen. It may be a long time before you see him again. Remember to thank him. You owe him a lot. He did not need to teach you. Without him you would not have come this far.' Akio went to sit nearby on a wooden stool as the crowd dispersed.

Ryo stepped across to speak to Unzen. Once he was standing in front of him, Ryo gave a deep formal bow, such as a pupil would give to a teacher in those times. 'Arigato, sensei,' he said. 'Thank you for your concern, your care and your instruction. I will do my best to be a credit to your teaching. I will always remember and respect the time I spent under your care.'

Unzen smiled quietly. 'Goodbye, Ryo. You have been a good pupil. There is much potential in you, I have noticed. You mean well. Now you must live and learn. From now on life will be your teacher. You will find her at times a tougher mistress than I was a master. Try to learn from all she shows you, regardless of how good or bad it may seem at the time. Don't dismiss anything. Whatever happens will teach you and help you to grow, provided you maintain the right attitude towards it. Try to remember this when things seem to be going badly. Go now, and may the Dragons of Air be behind you with their powers.'

Unzen bowed to him and Ryo returned the bow. As Ryo turned away he saw a large, stout fellow of about his own age gesture to him to approach. He stepped over to him uncertainly.

'Hi,' said the young man cheerfully. He was big and carried a lot of weight, but his face cracked into a broad grin and he almost seemed to be laughing, though not at Ryo. It was as if he found everything amusing. Ryo felt a wave of pleasure wash over him from the big fellow's warm presence.

'My name is Daiki,' he said, still beaming broadly. He gave the standard bow of introduction which Ryo returned.

'And I am Ryo,' Ryo replied. He waited to be told more.

'You are to come with me,' said Daiki. 'I'll show you where you're to live for the time being. And I'll tell you a little about us on the way.'

Ryo fell in with him and began to walk away from the large hall. As he did so he saw Akio and Unzen talking seriously together. They seemed to be discussing something important but he could not tell what.

Well, he was now at the next stage of training and his duty was to pursue that as best he could. Not for him to question the concerns of the leaders. He still had a lot to learn.

'We'll go to the hut now and I'll introduce you to the others,' said his new companion cheerfully.

There was something about Daiki that Ryo immediately took to. He was big and chunky with a solid feel to him, and he wore it well. He seemed to bear an aura of warmth and friendliness around him that was difficult to resist. It took you up in itself so that just being in his company made you feel happier and easier. Ryo found himself thinking that he was lucky to be in the same group as this fellow.

As they walked through the camp they passed numerous huts with mixed groups. Each hut seemed to house four or five people, boys and girls, men and women, mostly of an age with each other. So some huts housed older groups, some younger. Around each hut there was a space with a fire, rather like at Unzen's hermitage, a clear area where cooking and resting and warming oneself could take place. There was also a rough wooden structure for drying laundry. Clearly each group looked after itself domestically and did its own cleaning and cooking and washing.

Daiki pointed all this out to Ryo as they walked through the camp, also adding, 'Everyone takes turns with tending the allotments where we grow most of our food. And of course, there are the animals to see to, the chickens, ducks, goats and pigs. We are almost self-sufficient here. It's important for us not to rely on the outside world for much. That would seriously limit our capability. So, as well as working at your training while here, you will also be a part-time farmer. Everyone shares that role.'

This made sense to Ryo, of course. Living with Unzen had instilled in him the importance of self-reliance, of looking after oneself in the world. What Daiki had just said seemed a logical extension of the values Ryo had already begun to learn on Cold Mountain.

As Daiki led Ryo into the small camp that was to be his home Ryo at once noticed two more people waiting. One was sitting quietly on a rough wooden stool doing nothing. He was lean and lithe and had a very serious look about him. While Daiki was warm and cheerful, this young man was dark and serious in his manner. As he saw Ryo arrive he stood up and made a curt, formal bow to him, looking at him very directly, as if reading his nature through his face.

'This is Katsuo,' said Daiki, completely unaffected by the young man's serious manner and unflinching gaze. 'He is a model student. He never gets anything wrong.'

'Perhaps,' murmured Katsuo in a low voice. 'But nobody is perfect . . .'

'And this is Ryo,' Daiki continued, his cheerful warmth unchanged by Katsuo's seriousness. 'So now we are four. A complete group at last.' He turned from Katsuo to point out a young girl who seemed to be dancing a few yards away.

As Ryo looked at her he found himself entranced by her movements. She was small and light and appeared to move on air. As Ryo watched her he began to recognize some of her positions as those he had learned from Unzen. But they were woven together in a kind of fluent dance, seamlessly flowing into one another and just occasionally pausing as she pivoted to turn.

As they approached her she froze mid-movement and fell into a normal stance. She smiled radiantly and gave them both the standard bow.

'This is Chou,' said Daiki. 'Don't be fooled by the name. It may mean "butterfly" but this is a butterfly made of fine steel. More of a dragonfly, you might say.'

Chou wagged a warning finger at Daiki. 'Mind your teasing, big boy,' she said, 'or this dragonfly might sting . . .'

'You see then,' said Daiki, 'what you are up against? One very serious student. One dangerous butterfly. And a great big clown who takes everything lightly. Can you fit in with us, do you think? Will we make a good team?'

Ryo wasn't sure what to say. For all of Daiki's lightness of manner, this was a real question. Would he fit in here? He wasn't really like any of the others. Maybe a little like Katsuo, perhaps, but Katsuo was somehow different in a way Ryo couldn't yet put his finger on. So he said the only thing he could under the circumstances.

'I will try,' said Ryo, hoping he didn't sound as lame in reply as he felt.

'Yokoso!' beamed Chou, showing her beautiful white teeth in a kind smile.

'Yokoso,' echoed Katsuo politely.

'Yokoso,' chuckled Daiki. 'Now you are one of us, for better or worse.'

'Yokoso' meant welcome and, for now, Ryo felt as welcome as he could expect among new people. He had arrived at the next stage of his training. He was among people of his own age with a shared purpose. And he was part of an organization he wished to learn more about. He could hardly complain.

CHAPTER ELEVEN

I cannot in a tale of this length give you an account of the full scope of the training that went on at the Hill Camp. It would require a full written manual with diagrams, techniques, philosophy and history. Even that would be incomplete, since so much of the training was transmitted directly from teacher to pupil, and that would be adapted by each teacher in the case of each pupil, according to the individual qualities of both teacher and pupil. This was built into the system and formed one of its essential strengths.

But the heart of that system you may have already grasped from my account of Ryo's time with Unzen. What Unzen was attempting to pass on to Ryo at the Cold Mountain Hermitage was the gist, the central essence, of the practice. Training at the Hill Camp would prove to be a building onto that foundation.

Speed, strength, agility and skills would be rehearsed and evolved, but at their core, and holding them together, would be the central principles that Unzen had been gradually instilling in Ryo from the start of his training. And those were principles of intention and attitude rather than matters of physical prowess and outward skill.

Living and studying at the Hill Camp involved an intense saturation in a culture that had been evolved across several centuries at least. There was far more to it than simply learning to fight with skill. That having been said, the fighting skills reached were perhaps the highest ever attained across human culture anywhere, anytime. But it was more than just fighting. There was the matter of living, of how best to live, of how to have one's being in whatever setting or circumstances one might find oneself. And for the Hidden Ones, 'circumstances' might equally mean a room one happened to walk into or the entire cosmos as far as human knowledge might embrace. So we are thinking big here, but flexibly also, and including the small and the narrow with the big and the wide. And the inner world of the person as well as the outer, along with the acknowledgement that those two aspects may be more interdependent than one might habitually think.

But already I am getting beyond myself. Having

pointed briefly to the nature of the culture into which Ryo had been dropped, let me continue with his story.

The discipline at the Hill Camp was surprisingly unmilitary, it turned out. True, there was regularity and order to each day. But there was nothing harsh, punitive or heartless about the tone of the place. People were pleasant to each other, polite, and there was good humour in their dealings with one another. There was a good natured sense of common purpose. And there were times to relax and chat and play a little.

On the second day of Ryo's time with his team, he found himself both entertained, yet informally instructed, by witnessing his three companions sparring with each other in their small camp space. They took turns to pair off and face each other in combat, the style being to make genuine moves while withholding blows to an absolute minimum force. This way, it was a 'real fight' in which no one was hurt, yet in which the moves were practised. The discipline of withholding force from blows also practised the art of fighting without feeling, of not allowing anger or aggression to enter one's fight. As any trained fighter knows, that is a sure way to lose one's mental balance and one's sharpness of judgement. One must fight, if one fights at all, with keen alertness yet with complete emotional detachment. In a way one must become bonded to one's adversary as if they were a dancing partner rather than an enemy. This can sound strange, yet it is true.

First Daiki paired with Katsuo. Katsuo had all the qualities of the classic martial artist. He was lean, fit and absolutely alert at all times. He was not of heavy build, but well-muscled enough and with supreme gymnastic and athletic skills. So he was fast and swift. Weighing him up, Ryo wondered if he would ever be able to match up to an opponent of Katsuo's calibre.

But Daiki, though slower through his bulk, had immense blocking ability. He had great weight which he could manoeuvre with grace and poise. And Ryo tried to imagine the force necessary to bring such a stalwart figure to the ground. He could use his great arms with enough speed to ward off blows with skill and firmness. Again, Ryo thought, how could he begin to manage an opponent so large and solid? It was just then that Katsuo performed a move that reminded Ryo of the way Akio had toppled the brigand in his village. It was just a matter of slipping into a position in which if one exerted maximum force one's opponent could be thrown off balance. Ah, Daiki was going down. It was amazing to see – one so big and firm toppled by one so much smaller and lighter. So it could be done! But look how Daiki curls and rolls into the fall, making minimum impact with the ground and is sitting up and laughing at his mistake and his loss of the bout.

And now Chou was dancing in to face Katsuo. Clearly, this game involved staying in as long as possible. As one partner was toppled to the ground, the next stepped in, and so on. So here was Chou, the little, pretty slip of a girl, confronting the serious and formidable Katsuo.

'Stop!' Ryo wanted to call out. 'This can't be right . . .' But he need not have worried, for as soon as Katsuo made a move towards her she seemed to melt into air and be somewhere else. She could dance around Katsuo like a sprite, as if goading and teasing him so that when he finally made a kick or a punch or a lunge she was elsewhere by the time his move would have contacted her. Yet Katsuo was skilled. He was no buffoon. So how could Chou read him so sharply? She evidently already knew his strengths and weaknesses, the kinds of move he tended to favour. And she must have developed her ability to predict an opponent's next move with lightning speed. Her own speed of movement, her balance, grace and poise, were weapons in their own right. And she was decisive in weaving them together in that fluid, seamless dance she could spin out at a moment's notice. And, yes, Katsuo was going down. Chou had lured him into pushing just fractionally beyond his balance point and he had to make a swift somersault to recover himself. But this meant he was down, if momentarily, so he was out of the bout. He grunted as he rose to his feet and stood back.

'You see!' called Daiki to Ryo who stood watching. 'It's like I said, no? The Steel Butterfly. Am I not right?'

'And you are the Giant Caterpillar,' quipped Chou. 'Can you crawl fast enough to catch me, though?' She giggled as she danced in front of him.

'Oh, enough,' groaned Daiki. 'I can never catch you. It's impossible. And I'm hungry now. Let's make supper.'

The previous evening Ryo had told his three new companions his story. So they now knew about Ryo's village, and of how he first encountered Akio. They had heard the tale of his journey to Cold Mountain to seek Unzen and of his apprenticeship there with him before being brought to the Hill Camp. As Ryo had told them his story he had, for the first time, the sense of being understood by people of his own age. He felt no need to explain his feelings, his urges, his ambitions. He could simply tell them the facts, with the sense that his intentions and hopes seemed to them entirely comprehensible.

This evening it was time for his new friends to tell their own tales. After supper they sat around the fire, taking it in turns.

Daiki, he learned, had lost his family when his village had been plundered and sacked by brigands.

A comrade of Akio had found him as a child in the smoking ruins of the village. He'd taken him to an orphanage supported by the Hidden Ones. As he showed a great interest in combat skills, when he was old enough he was allowed to come and study at the Hill Camp. He felt lucky to have survived. And it was clear that at some level he wanted to be prepared in the future to face up to the kinds of people who had sacked his village and killed his family. Beneath his open-hearted cheerfulness there was a more serious purpose.

Katsuo was the son of a samurai, a professional soldier. His father had got caught up in a complex system of feuds between warring clans. This had led to his assassination, which Katsuo had witnessed as a young boy. The experience had led him to abhor conflict and violence of any kind. Yet it had also induced in him a sense of the need for an individual to be able to protect himself and others should the situation arise. In a deep sense it was as if he wanted the ability to be able to save his father, even though his father was now long dead. Harsh experience can have such a formative effect on us, especially when we are young. Katsuo told of how, during martial arts training, he had come across the rumour of a hill camp in the Great Waste where one could get the best training possible. Just as Ryo had sought out his hermit on Cold Mountain, Katsuo had sought out the Hill Camp.

Through great perseverance he had finally found it. After close interviewing and assessment the Hill Camp had allowed him entry and training.

Ryo saw something of himself in Katsuo, though Katsuo's darker, more brooding side made Ryo feel uneasy. Katsuo seemed somehow damaged by his early experience, which was hardly surprising. It gave him a locked-off, slightly hostile and obsessive quality. He lacked . . . ah, that was it! thought Ryo, he lacked tenderness. There was something rigid and uncreative about him, though his fighting moves had a machine-like invincibility about them. Ryo doubted he could ever match up to an adversary as technically skilled as Katsuo. Yet he felt he already had understandings that Katsuo might lack. He wondered if Katsuo ever saw beauty in anything, which he, Ryo, the son of a potter, evidently did.

Which brings us to Chou, in whom Ryo had at once seen beauty, almost to gasping point, not least when he had witnessed her magical dancing combat style. He found himself watching her much of the time, simply for the fluidity of her movements, whether she was in fighting mode or just stirring a pot or carrying something across their small compound. She had poise and dignity yet sometimes her face would crack into a smile to reveal an impish sense of humour and a wicked playfulness.

She did not know her origins. She'd been told that she'd been abandoned as an infant, left out by her family to die on a mountainside. The people she'd been born to sometimes did that with unwanted girl children. It was thought to be unlucky to have too many girls, both in a family and in the wider tribe, so surplus girl babies were simply left out to die in the wild. Mostly they died quickly of exposure and were eaten as carrion by foxes or crows. But Chou had been found quite by chance, rather like Daiki. She too had been raised in the orphanage, along with Daiki. They had become like cousins, so when Daiki was invited to go to the Hill Camp, Chou had asked to go with him. Her natural and unusual combat skill was soon noticed by the teachers and she had acquired a reputation amongst her age group for her original style. It was sometimes whispered, Daiki had murmured to Ryo already, that Chou might one day develop a whole new school of self-defence technique built around her personal style. This might suit people who were by nature small, light and thereby potentially swift and agile, rather than strong, muscled and solid.

Ryo soon settled into the routine of the Hill Camp. He had much to learn and was not yet able to enter combat play with his three companions. It was acknowledged that he'd need to attend the daily training sessions for some time before he'd be in any way on a level with them. But he fitted in well and came to be happy in their company. It was like having a family, which was a comfort. And it provided a balance from the more formal daily training sessions where large groups exercised and practised under the attentive gaze of the teachers. The teachers were older men and women who had risen through the ranks of the Hill Camp to become trainers of the younger members. All had their individual stories, the blends of fate and chance by which they'd found their way through the Great Waste to be members of this unique society.

It was an average day of training and Daiki, Katsuo, Chou and Ryo were assembled expectantly in front of Akio. Other such groups were dotted about across the training ground, mostly with four pupils to one trainer. Ryo felt privileged to note that his family group were to be instructed personally by Akio. But Akio was beginning to address them so he focused his attention carefully on what was being said.

'As you know, our fighting method is in essence defensive rather than aggressive. This means that a central part of our art is one of disarming an attacker, where the attacker is bearing a weapon and the defender is initially unarmed. I say "initially" because of course we all need to know how to handle weapons with utmost skill, though mostly we refrain from carrying them. When necessary we must be ready to disarm an attacker and use their weapon against them, with as much or more skill than they, themself, could wield it. This is why at other times we practise swordplay, archery, stave fighting and such.'

Akio scanned the young, listening faces before him to read their level of attention, then resumed. 'Today we are going to demonstrate responding to a sword attack. Clearly it would be foolish at this stage to use real swords so we will begin by substituting padded sticks.' A ripple of relief fanned across his listeners. 'Also you will wear padded jackets for the exercise. There will be many blows landing on your bodies and this will reduce bruising.' He pointed behind him to indicate a neat pile of jackets and four padded sticks, each the length of a samurai sword.

'Katsuo and Chou will demonstrate for us.' At his words the two companions stepped forward. They both donned jackets and Akio beckoned to Katsuo to pick up a stick.

Under Akio's instruction the two demonstrators took up positions on a slight downward slope. Katsuo, the attacker, stood above, looking down. Chou, the defender, stood below, adopting an alert, defensive stance that Ryo recognized as the basic, neutral stance of Hill Camp technique. Daiki nudged Ryo and pointed, to show how she had adjusted her position slightly, to compensate for the slope she was standing on. For her this adjustment appeared instinctive. Ryo noted it consciously. He recalled Unzen telling him how practise and rehearsal lead gradually to automaticity, and in that way how learned skills become natural habits.

At a nod from Akio Chou's attacker, Katsuo, bore down on her, stick raised, as if to deliver a classic blow to the neck. She ducked and the stick missed.

Akio called out, 'Halt!' And the two combatants froze in position.

'Now,' said Akio, turning to Daiki and Ryo. 'We can all manage a duck like that. We've practised it before. But watch again.' He turned and muttered a few words to Katsuo and Chou then stepped away as they returned to their original positions to start again.

This time, when Katsuo had cut and Chou had ducked, Katsuo recovered his missed stroke and in one fluent movement whirled round in a complete circle that did not interrupt the momentum his cut had gathered. He used his missed cut to his advantage, catching Chou on the calf with his padded stick. And there they froze again for the others to assess.

'Aha!' cried Akio dramatically. 'What now? Chou has a cut to the leg. She may be unable to fight on. What might she have done?'

The students' faces looked serious. None came forward with an immediate solution but all seemed to be working it through in their minds' eyes.

Akio took Chou aside and murmured quietly to her, demonstrating with hand movements as he spoke. She nodded thoughtfully. Ryo noted how quickly she seemed to catch on to Akio's directions.

'Go again,' Akio called to his two demonstrators.

Katsuo prepared to repeat his attack as Chou resumed neutral position. Down came the cut. And there went Chou's duck, so deft. Ryo marvelled at Katsuo's whirl, like a dance, and . . . but where was Chou? Katsuo's second cut to the calf met thin air and he whirled on round just recovering himself from losing balance. Chou, having ducked, had rolled away to one side and backward, removing her from the reach of the whirling sword. Her roll finished in a neat rise to her feet, facing her unbalanced attacker once more. A gasp of admiration and delight came from both Daiki and Ryo.

Akio commented swiftly. 'Katsuo, of course, guessed the move that was coming. A less smart swordfighter would have been thrown off balance and might even have gone down. That would have given Chou time to be at them, possibly, or even to seize their sword, which they might have dropped. At the least, Chou would be unharmed and ready for the next move from her attacker. The more a fight like this goes on, of course, the more a skilled defender will be reading the attacker's moves and gauging their style and habit. This way advantage can be gained as a fight proceeds, enabling the defender at last to disarm and disable their attacker. So, watch just once more and then I shall ask you all to try Chou's moves.'

Daiki and Ryo watched again as the sequence was repeated.

Then Akio instructed, 'Take turns now in attacking and defending, in pairs. Repeat the sequence and aim for a seamless series of movements throughout.'

Daiki and Ryo jacketed up, and the two pairs spread out across the slope and took their positions. There was an atmosphere of intense concentration. As action commenced, the focus was only punctuated by the occasional grunt or gasp, the swish of sticks in the air and the thud of sticks meeting their targets. Now and then a dull thump indicated someone falling heavily to the ground.

'Soft landings!' Akio reminded the students with evident good humour.

From time to time one pair would stop altogether to huddle with Akio who would then speak to them in low, swift tones, manipulating them into position and directing their movement like a choreographer with dancers.

In this way, day by day, week by week, the students honed their skills, becoming gradually more accomplished in the combat methods of the Hidden Ones. Sometimes, as they worked together, a student's problem with a move would generate discussion and experiment, and the teaching and learning process would itself evolve new tricks and techniques.

At such times Akio would remind them, 'It is never finished, this business. You must never expect to arrive at a final stage of being the perfectly accomplished fighter. It is like being a musician. You must endlessly practise. The day you stop practising is the day you begin to fade in skill. However experienced you become there will always be the possibility of something completely unexpected to take you by surprise in a new way. Persistence, practice and an ever-open mind are essentials to anyone who reckons to walk this path.'

Chapter Twelve

As the months passed Ryo's skills developed considerably. He worked hard at his training and bit by bit he built on the basic foundations set down for him by Unzen on Cold Mountain.

Yet he began to experience a slight unease when he compared himself to his three companions. They were each unique, different, individual in their fighting styles. He could not yet imagine squaring up to any of them in one-on-one combat. He could not possibly match them. He had solid basic skills that would stand him in good stead on any village street, yet he had not yet found a distinctive style of his own, a style that reached into his own essential nature, as the others already had. What was his essential nature? Did he have one? How could he discover it? To Ryo his three companions seemed so distinctive, so well defined, so clear in outline. Yet when he contemplated himself all he could make out was a kind of blurry shape with no clear character.

Would he ever, he thought, be like them? Would he ever come into focus as a fighter and be able to stand his own ground alongside them? How might this be achieved? And how would he know if it was happening?

He never spoke of these doubts to them. But once a week he had to discuss his progress with his counsellor and he voiced his doubts there. His counsellor was a mature man, old enough, easily, to be his father. When you saw your counsellor you were supposed to talk frankly about your own sense of your progress, to talk realistically about how you thought things were going for you. They would question you and sometimes offer advice or suggestion. When Ryo talked of his sense of inadequacy in comparison to his companions the counsellor held up his hand in a gesture that caused Ryo to pause. There was a short silence in which the counsellor seemed to be collecting his thoughts. Then he spoke to Ryo steadily and seriously.

'You will never see your own clear outline in the way you see that of others. To you, others have a sense of definition, of clear character, of distinct nature or identity. To others, you will have something of that kind for them, though you do not see it yourself. You cannot separate yourself from yourself to see yourself as others may see you. You have to live from within yourself, remaining, in a sense, behind your own eyes, your own senses. Inside yourself, through meditation, as you will already have learned, it is possible to detach somewhat from thoughts, emotions and sense impressions and in that way you are able to observe the way your mind works, to see what a monkey the mind can be. That is the best way, the only reliable way, to "see yourself". And it is a good skill to have practised when it comes to fighting, for it helps you to detach emotionally from combat and simply practise it as a skill in itself. That way the emotions stay calm, the mind is still, yet the body is entirely active.'

The counsellor paused and looked searchingly into Ryo's face. Then he resumed. 'As to the matter of matching up to others in skill itself, there is only one course to take there. You simply practise, breath by breath, blow by blow, move by move. Each moment, each session, each day, and so on. Take your gaze off the distant mountain you seek to conquer and look down at your feet and make sure each step is sure and true. It is necessary occasionally to ensure your direction is good, that you are headed the right way for your purpose. But as to worrying when you will get there, how fast, or whether you will ever reach the high summit, that is mind energy wasted, mind space cluttered with unnecessary baggage. Throw it out.

Don't bother with it. When you catch yourself dwelling on such things just note it, let it go, take a deep breath and smile at your own small folly that as human beings we are all prone to. Don't berate yourself over it. Be kind to yourself. But learn to let it go and breathe. Just practise that. And work hard at your training.'

The counsellor paused again, drew himself in, took a deep breath and continued. 'There is just one more thing worth saying about all this. Don't be alarmed by it, but bear it in mind for the future. Whatever one is doing, whatever course one has chosen for oneself, no matter how driven one has felt to undertake it, this can always change. However committed you have been to no matter what cause or purpose, a time may come when you feel differently, you decide differently and your values change along with your direction in life. This can happen to anyone. We are not fixed. We do not learn our own nature and then engage it. Rather, through what we do, through what we have done, we learn gradually what our nature might be. This fluidity, this uncertainty, goes on until we die. And who can say what happens after that?

'It is even possible, no matter what you now think or feel, that you are not cut out to be a fighter after all.' On hearing this Ryo flinched slightly but he knew better than to interrupt his counsellor. And this was not an idea that he wanted to consider.

'Your direction may one day turn. Perhaps you will be a monk, or a merchant, or even a potter like your father. No one can yet say, not even you.

'I've spoken enough,' the counsellor rounded off. 'It's time to go and eat your supper. Eat it gratefully and remember to wash your bowl.' He bowed formally to Ryo who returned the bow. He then struck the small bell by his right knee. With the sound of the bell ringing in his ears Ryo got up from his sitting cushion and left the counselling hut.

It was not long after this meeting that the four companions were called as a group to see Akio. They were sitting quietly together having just finished a sparring session. Soon they would cook supper for themselves, but they were regaining their breath. At Katsuo's suggestion Ryo had begun to spar with them. For several sessions now he had joined in and done his best to level up to each of them. So far he had not beaten any of the three, but already he could hold out longer than at first and he was beginning to learn their individual styles, their habits and methods. Though he could not beat them yet he could often predict how they were going to beat him, even though he was not yet quick or skilled enough to prevent it from happening. But being in actual combat with them and learning to read their movements and to assess his own responses was teaching him well. He had got over his initial inhibitions and nervousness about sparring with them and already had developed a keen spirit to engage. The more he practised the more this grew in him. He felt truly one of the group at last. He felt integrated and 'on his way'.

But now they were resting after the session when a young girl entered their area.

'I have a message for you from Akio,' she said aloud to them all.

'Say away,' said Daiki to her with characteristic cheerfulness.

The others focused on the girl with curiosity. A message from Akio was an unusual thing. What could this be about?

'He says he wants to see you in the morning after breakfast. He wants all four of you to go as a group. He has something he wants to tell you. That is the message. That's all I know. Thank you.' The girl bowed quickly and turned to leave.

'And thank you for the message.' Daiki spoke for the group but the girl had gone before his words were out.

'I wonder what this will be about . . .' murmured Chou, half to herself, though the others could hear her well enough.

'Have we slipped up, do you think?' suggested Daiki.

'Foolish to wonder,' said Katsuo sharply. 'It could be anything, good or bad or neither. Better to wait and find out than to speculate aimlessly.' He shook his head disapprovingly.

'Still . . .' persisted Chou, undaunted. 'I can't help wondering.'

Ryo said nothing. He was reading his companions as he often did, noticing their different ways of responding to situations. They were each so different from each other.

'It'll be me,' groaned Daiki. 'He'll say I'm getting too fat for a fighter. He'll tell you to control my diet. It'll be hungry days ahead for me. Half portions with no treats.' He rubbed his belly and made a miserable face.

Chou and Ryo laughed and even Katsuo shot him a glance that might have contained a glimmer of amusement.

'Tomorrow we'll know,' said Katsuo thoughtfully.

And tomorrow they did know. As they sat respectfully in front of Akio he told them about the challenge mission he was sending them on.

'There is a village about two days' journey from here,' he said, looking from face to face to read their reactions. 'It is a small, poor place where the villagers scratch out a living for themselves by hard work and thrift. They are humble people who live close to the earth and have little to spare.'

The four companions sat silently, listening to his words carefully. They knew already that this was a mission of some kind that they were about to be sent on. From time to time groups such as theirs were sent out on challenge missions. These were real situations that needed addressing, usually out there in the world but not too far from the Hill Camp. When a problem arose that might be solved by the skills of the Hidden Ones a young group would be sent out to deal with it as best they could. This was a way of giving them an opportunity to harness the skills they had acquired and apply them in the real world out there beyond the sphere of the camp. It meant facing real danger and risking one's safety or even one's life.

'They are being preyed upon,' continued Akio, 'by a small group of brigands. Three in number, from the information I have received. These brigands are making frequent visits to bully provisions from the villagers. They never pay for what they take and they take more than the villagers can spare. The villagers themselves are beginning to go hungry due to this situation. But the brigands have no compassion. If they milk the village dry then they will simply move on to another village and try their tricks there. Your task in this case is to travel to the village and befriend the villagers. Tell them your intention is to merge in with them in order to combat the brigands when they next visit. If they seem unconvinced by your ability to be of use to them, just say you represent the Hidden Ones. Enough rumour and legend surrounds us in those parts to persuade them that your aptitude will match that of their roguish visitors.'

Katsuo had raised his hand.

Akio addressed him directly. 'You have a question, Katsuo?'

'Yes, master,' said Katsuo seriously. 'We will almost certainly come into direct combat with the brigands at some point. If we do so, do we fight "with full intent"?'

'With full intent.' This was a phrase that meant, should it become necessary, one might kill one's opponent in combat in order to bring things to conclusion. Wherever possible the code of the Hidden Ones avoided killing. The object was to resist wrong with skilful force but to give the wrongdoer future opportunity to mend their ways once justice had been meted out. But in cases where an opponent was bent on maintaining or reviving combat to the point of threatening death to others, then it was deemed necessary to end the situation by killing them as swiftly and efficiently as possible.

'You should be able,' said Akio insistently, 'to overcome them with the skills you already have. Your instructions are that once this is achieved you will truss them safely and leave them in the hands of the villagers so that they can be delivered up to a local marshal in the nearest town.'

Akio made it clear that he was speaking to the whole group when he said this and, Katsuo's question dealt with, he continued with further detail. 'I am sending along with you one of our trainers, Azami. She will travel with you as your potential supporter and adviser should things go badly wrong for you. She is, as you will know, as highly skilled in judgement as in combat. You will already have encountered her in training sessions so she will not be a stranger. However, do not regard her as your group leader. She will travel alongside you and be nearby you at all times during your mission. But she will only intervene if your lives are seriously at risk. This challenge is for you to meet yourselves, as a group of four. She will be assessing how you conduct yourselves. She will meet with you briefly before you set off. Any questions of detail can be covered with her then. She has performed this role before so you will find her an experienced adviser.'

Akio paused, then looked at Ryo. 'Ryo,' he said quietly, 'I am aware that you do not yet match your companions equally in combat skills. There is no shame in that. But I want to make clear that if you are outmatched in combat the others will be looking out for you. And this includes your adviser, Azami.

You are skilful enough, mostly, to look after yourself defensively. But be sure to engage in direct combat only when at least one of the others is to hand for support. Is that clear?'

'Yes, master,' replied Ryo respectfully. He had a flash of memory in which he saw himself as a young boy pestering Akio on the hill track, begging him to take him and train him in the skills of fighting. And now here he was, about to set out on his first mission, instructed by his hero, Akio. He felt a momentary surge of exuberance.

As the four companions left the hall where the meeting with Akio had taken place they walked in silence for a while. Each seemed caught up in their own thoughts. It was Daiki who broke the silence.

'So I'm not to be on a diet then. That's a relief.'

The others seemed to welcome this note of good humour. They came out of their brooding and smiled. Even Katsuo's lips twisted upwards for a moment before he remembered to be dignified and serious. But it was Chou who responded.

'Even so, I think you should be on half rations for the journey there. That way you will be nimble for the action.'

'No, I should have half of yours as butterflies need so little nourishment for their skinny frames. That would be fair.'

'This butterfly needs extra energy for her lightning speed, though, and she's quick enough to steal some of yours while it's on its way to your mouth. So watch out, Snail's Pace!'

The humorous banter stopped abruptly there, for they had arrived in front of Azami's hut, their next place to call. Hearing them arrive she emerged from the dark frame of the doorway and greeted them.

'No point in delaying. We have the rest of today to prepare. We can leave early in the morning. We'll sleep out in the open for one night on the way. We should be there by the middle of the following day. We travel light. We should not need to be there long. Take as much in the way of provisions as is practical. The villagers are short of food as it is. But hopefully we will put that to rights.'

Azami knew all four of the companions already. She had been involved in some of their training sessions so had a clear idea of their skills and aptitudes. She herself was known to be sharply clever and very swift. She had more weight than Chou, as a female fighter, so her skills were more along orthodox lines. But she too had a lightness and speed which, under the right conditions, could get the better of a much heavier and more muscled opponent. As ever, the method taught one to make the best of one's natural attributes, to go with what one had got rather than to work oneself into something else. That way much energy was saved. And much time too.

'I'm not going to talk plans and strategies with you, in case you were wondering about that. This mission is yours to accomplish. I will be there to watch your progress. I'll only get directly involved if things become extremely dangerous for you. So don't expect me to take over at the slightest hitch. I am a last resort. You are meant to solve this problem yourselves, through your individual skills and combined resourcefulness. That is what a challenge mission is for.'

The four companions were given time that afternoon to prepare their travel bundles and provisions for the next few days and to discuss with each other their initial plan of action. This would probably change, it was understood, once they were there, according to the way they found things on arrival. But it seemed good to weigh up their various abilities and to agree on some basic strategies.

Daiki, being the largest and physically strongest, should be able to front up to an opponent face to face and use his power to block or even to overwhelm.

Katsuo could come into his own if it came to skilful, balanced martial art of a classic kind, though it seemed unlikely a brigand would excel at such a thing. But better to be prepared. An opponent might turn out to be well trained in some such way.

Chou would use speed to distract and confuse, though if necessary she could seize weapons and turn them on their owners too. She was very dextrous at such tricks. She could also initially use surprise, as any stranger to her would not expect her to be in command of the skills she had. She could seem like a sweet young girl. In a way she was that too. Yet what hidden talents she could call on.

But what of Ryo? Ah, Ryo . . . well, he must find his chances to use the skills he had to cover the backs of the others should they be threatened from behind or obliquely. And like Chou he could distract by presenting himself as a second adversary if any of his companions seemed to be struggling. He could also be there to protect villagers from the conflict coming their way. The group did not wish to create casualties among any bystanders.

That evening they prepared a simple meal and then sat round the fire for a while, murmuring to each other about the coming mission. Beneath their talk was a serious vein of concern. This would be their first real encounter of such a kind. There was always the possibility that real injury or even death might be involved. This was no game. And blows would be for real now. They said their goodnights in due course and turned in early. They wanted to be up with first light.

Before he went to sleep Ryo reassured himself

that they would be in the company of Azami. It was rumoured around the camp that when the time came for Akio to step down or move on from leadership Azami would be his most likely successor. She had all the qualities required to be a leader of the Hidden Ones. Such a post was regarded as a responsibility rather than a privilege. One needed extreme combat skills honed to the sharpest edge, yet tempered with intelligent understanding of human nature and emotional relations. Azami seemed to have the perfect balance of these complementary skills. So Ryo reassured himself that should things go wrong there would at least be a skilled elder supporter to fend for the four young companions.

Their journey was swift and uneventful. They practised the art of silent travelling often used by the Hidden Ones when conducting a mission. This involved a form of rapid, mindful walking. The emphasis was more on not delaying than on hurrying. And one occupied one's mind simply by taking in one's surroundings, noticing where one was headed and what was around one. That way anything untoward would be spotted as soon as possible. By not chatting or singing or daydreaming one would be least likely to bring attention to the group from anyone coming the other way or waiting in the vicinity. It reminded Ryo of his journey to the Hill Camp with Unzen, as did the way they pitched camp overnight near a stream and with tree cover available. They made up their makeshift beds, drank water from the stream and did without a fire so as, again, to leave little trace of their having stayed there. They ate modestly from their cold rations and restricted their talk to essential business. Ryo noticed that Azami remained at a distance from them as she had on the journey. There she had walked behind them, about thirty paces or so. Here, likewise, she made up her bed at a similar distance from them. Anyone looking on would have assumed she was not a member of the group, but simply someone travelling with them at close proximity.

Their sleep was sound but short. A day's silent walking used a lot of energy, which needed restoring. But a sparse bed on the ground did not invite long sleep. As they rose they all performed warming and stretching exercises that were routine for them, though more necessary after a night out of doors. They washed in the stream and took a light breakfast from their packs. Once that was done they were away again, with Azami taking up the rear at the same measured distance.

In due course, as midday approached, they found themselves walking between cultivated fields where crops were grown. Some were paddy fields, for rice. Others were clearly for root vegetables of various kinds. They made out a single figure in the distance, ploughing with a bullock. And soon, further along the track, they could distinguish thatched huts. This was surely the village.

They had already agreed on an initial stratagem the day before leaving the Hill Camp. Katsuo would speak to the heads of the village, introducing the four companions and their senior as members of the Hidden Ones. He would ask that they be allowed to pass themselves off as members of the village. If the brigands commented on not having seen them before, this could be covered by them being visitors, come to the village to assist relatives, joining in with tasks and labour as was sometimes the custom. Katsuo would explain to the village heads that the four of them, with Azami overlooking, would find opportunity to overcome and secure the three brigands to be delivered up to the local marshal by the villagers themselves.

As the four companions entered the village they were eyed with uncertainty and suspicion to begin with. Who were these interlopers? The villagers were now used to daily visitations from the bandits, but these four young people looked in no way like bandits. Besides, the bandits had already visited that morning and had gone away with fresh provisions for themselves to their camp which lay through the forest and up the hill. They would not be back until tomorrow. So who were these youngsters? And who was that older woman who seemed to be keeping her distance from them, yet had arrived just behind them?

Katsuo approached one of the villagers, an old man wearing a straw hat and holding a staff to support himself.

'Tell me, sir. Where are the village elders to be found? I need to speak to them.'

The old man raised a thin arm and pointed with a bony finger to a hut that lay just across the compound. 'Over there,' he said in a shaky voice. 'In that hut. They are drinking tea, I think.'

Katsuo beckoned to his companions to come with him as he walked towards the hut. The others followed. Azami had sat down on the ground across the compound against the rough wall of a hut.

The doorway to the elders' hut was open. Katsuo knocked on the doorpost three times and waited for a response.

'Please enter,' came a voice from within.

Katsuo had to adjust his eyes to the gloom as he entered. His companions also had trouble seeing clearly at first. As their eyes adjusted to the dim light they saw four villagers, two men and two women, sitting behind a charcoal fire. Before them were rough tea bowls and a metal teapot on a stand. When they saw Katsuo and his three companions one of them clapped loudly and a young boy appeared.

'More bowls,' said the woman who had clapped. 'Four guests, four bowls, quickly.'

She beckoned to Katsuo to sit. As he did so the other three sat down behind him so that it was clear he was the spokesperson for them. The boy set down bowls in front of them then brought the metal pot and filled each bowl with hot liquid. As the scent from the bowls rose they could tell that this was wheat tea. Villagers such as this could not afford real tea, cha, unless they were growing it themselves. Even then, it would be a commercial crop, so prized for sale and rarely to be consumed by the villagers themselves. Wheat tea was what the Hidden Ones mainly drank as their hot beverage back at the Hill Camp, again, for reasons of economy. But it was welcome hospitality and they drank it gratefully.

'What brings you here?' said the old woman. 'We get few visitors in these parts.' It was clear she was the senior of the elders. Probably the oldest in years and thereby the most venerated. Though old she still had her wits about her and appeared to have a wiry strength resulting from years of regular physical work in the open air.

'My name is Katsuo. These are my companions, Daiki, Chou and Ryo. Outside in the compound is Azami, our adviser and teacher. We have been sent here to rid your village of bandits . . .'

When the elders heard this they exchanged glances that might have been interpreted as incredulous.

'You are young,' said one of the men. 'And you bear no weapons. You look more like peasants than warriors. How do you propose to achieve this feat?'

'We may look young,' replied Katsuo with confidence. 'But we are well trained. We have advanced fighting skills. And our adviser is yet more proficient. Our information is that there are only three bandits in the group who extort provisions from you. The four of us should be equal to the task. If not, I am confident our adviser will step in to support us. She is of the best.'

'But how did you come to know of our problem? And where do you come from? How is it that you have found us?' This was the second man speaking now.

'We are from the Hidden Ones,' replied Katsuo, with a note of pride in his voice. 'Perhaps you have heard of us. One of our agents brought news of your problem back to our leader. It is our leader who has sent us on this mission. This is a challenge we are eager to fulfil.'

At this mention of the Hidden Ones the leader of the elders raised her eyebrows and talked in a low voice to the others. Then she raised her head towards Katsuo and said, 'Thank you. We are satisfied by what you tell us. Please understand that we must be wary. Were you not up to the task this could make matters worse

141

for us. If the brigands thought we were assisting you in challenging them, as we will be by harbouring you here, then there would be fierce reprisals. They would kill some, if not all, of us as punishment, should you fail in your task.'

'We understand that,' said Katsuo. 'But even at the worst the Hidden Ones would send a second group to deal with the brigands and *they* would certainly not fail. Without our help your village, as we understand, will be gradually bled of resources. These men will eventually have taken all you have and will leave you destitute before moving on to another village. So we urge you to take our help and be rid of these parasites.' Katsuo spoke that last sentence with a vehemence that clearly convinced the elders.

The fourth, the woman who had not yet spoken, addressed him. 'So what do you propose, young man?'

Katsuo paused, took a breath, then spoke quickly. 'Our aim is to blend in with the other villagers. Should the brigands notice our newness we can be explained as relatives come from a neighbouring village to help with the workload. We will indeed contrive to be working alongside you when the brigands arrive to take provisions and whatever else they intend. That way we can observe them in order to weigh up their capabilities before challenging them directly. Rest assured, we are trained in such things. For us this is an opportunity to test ourselves. We are equal to the challenge.'

The elders nodded approvingly. They seemed convinced by Katsuo's reassurances. The senior elder clapped loudly again and the boy reappeared from behind her.

'Take our guests,' she said to him. 'Show them to the guest house and see they are comfortable. Make sure they are given what they need for the night. And fetch your father. I will tell him to alert the other villagers to the situation. We must all behave as if nothing unusual is happening. Our friends here must have the full advantage of surprise. That way fewer casualties are likely.'

Katsuo nodded to her approvingly. The old woman clearly had her wits about her. Their plan was to go ahead. Now they simply had to keep themselves alert and focused, ready for the confrontation the next day.

As they were shown to their quarters Chou spoke. 'Well done, Katsuo. You were very persuasive. You impressed the elders, which will make our task more straightforward.'

The following day the four companions were up and breakfasted early. Before leaving their hut they sat in silence together, preparing their minds and bodies for the challenge that lay ahead.

Katsuo eventually broke the silence. 'We must not

be complacent,' he said. 'They may be brigands, but one or all of them may have had training in fighting arts. It would not be the first time a trained warrior had turned to the bad.'

'I have seen brigands before,' said Ryo. 'Back in my village when I was still a boy. They were armed like samurai. But it was Akio they came up against, so it looked like they were incompetent fighters. But then Akio is one of the best, and none of us could equal his skills.'

'But we are four,' Chou cut in. 'We are one-to-one plus one extra,' she said, nodding to Ryo. 'And we may be able to pick them off one at a time if we are clever or lucky.'

'Best not to reckon on luck at such a time,' said Daiki wisely. For once he was level-headed and serious. This was no time for lightness and he knew it.

The previous night the companions had made arrangements with the villagers to be in the central compound at the expected time of the brigands' arrival. The villagers were to bring out their tool sharpening equipment so that their visitors could appear to be cleaning, sharpening and mending a collection of farm tools. They could make a convincing show of this as it was a task they had all performed many a time at the Hill Camp. Already they had heard several villagers setting this up for them in preparation. It seemed time now to go and make a start, keeping an eye out for the brigands. Two villagers were watching out for them so as to alert them when they could be seen coming along the track towards the village. The villagers had been cautioned to appear as natural as possible and to do nothing out of the ordinary, so that the brigands would not be on their guard against anything untoward.

The four companions set about their work, gently and nonchalantly, not wasting unnecessary effort yet performing their tasks convincingly enough. Every now and then they would pause briefly and look around them, so as to take in the nature of their immediate setting: who was where, who was doing what, what obstacles and objects were in the compound, what animals . . . and so forth.

Eventually one of the lookouts sauntered over to them and hissed, 'They are on their way. They will be here in a few minutes.'

Daiki stood up and feigned mopping his brow. As he did so he took in the sight of the three approaching figures. Though still a few minutes away he could make them out. He paused just long enough to read their movements before turning back to his apparent work.

'One big one,' he murmured to his friends. 'Armed like a samurai. A sword, a belt dagger and a spear. He swaggers. But he looks slow. One taller but thin. He looks mean and he could be agile. A lighter sword and probably a dagger also. One shorter, stouter, but probably strong in arm and with much vigour about him. I could not make out his weapons. Not easy opponents. Not a pushover. So we must be on our mettle.' As he spoke the other three took opportunities to glance surreptitiously at the approaching men who had by now neared since Daiki had begun his summary.

In their simple tunics the four young friends looked like plain villagers, so unless they did anything to provoke the brigands they need not attract undue attention from them. This would give the companions time to choose an apt moment to begin combat. For now, though, they focused on their tasks again in order to look like villagers at work.

Very shortly the three brigands swaggered into the compound.

'What's this?' said the big one, the one dressed as a samurai. 'Tool sharpening! Ideal. Just the thing. You can sharpen my spear while you're at it.' He said this to Daiki who was sharpening a sickle on a foot-operated whetstone.

Daiki looked up at him with that good-natured, open smile of his. 'Why, certainly, sir. I'll do it right now.' He put the sickle aside and took the spear from the big man. 'I could do your sword too while I'm at it . . . and your dagger too. Kill three birds with one whetstone, so to speak . . .'

'Oh, yes, very good. A comedian. But don't get too clever, or I might have to cut you down to size,' said the brigand putting his sword down on the bench and stepping back to allow Daiki to do the work.

'That would be difficult . . .' replied Daiki, still smiling, 'without your sword and spear.' As he said this, with sudden speed he tossed the spear to Ryo, who was standing nearby, apparently cleaning a hoe. As Ryo caught it mid shaft he saw Daiki snatch up the sword from the bench and level it at the man's throat.

With a fighter's instinct the big man stepped back and drew his dagger. As he did so he growled, half at Daiki, half to his two comrades, 'Upstart! This young puppy needs a lesson. Finish him.'

As Daiki squared up to the big man Ryo observed that though Daiki carried less bulk than his opponent he was a good match for him in size. Being younger he also fared to outmatch him in agility, though agility was not Daiki's strong point.

But now the brigand's accomplices were advancing, on their guard. They could see that Daiki held the sword while their fellow had only his dagger.

Ryo edged round and thrust the spear towards the lean, mean-looking brigand who had drawn his sword.

'Get back,' he warned. 'This combat is for two only right now.'

The mean one leered at Ryo who held the spear firmly levelled towards the man's stomach. 'Will you throw it or thrust it then?' he taunted. 'Make your move . . .'

But Ryo did not need to make his move for out of the blue Katsuo came at the man from the side wielding a hoe. He brought the iron end of the hoe down smartly on the man's sword hand so the sword fell to the ground and he grimaced in pain. His other hand reached instinctively for his dagger.

Two handed fighter! thought Ryo in a flash. Need to beware of that. As he thought that, he saw Katsuo scoop the man's sword aside with the hoe towards a nearby villager who picked it up and withdrew to a safer distance.

The stout man was slower to enter the fray. He had been distracted by Chou's good looks right from the start. He had turned his attention to her and had begun to sidle up to her in a provocative way. She had eluded his grasp with her characteristic moves in a way that at first baffled him and then began to annoy him. So when his big comrade called out, he was unprepared for the combat that was already beginning. As he turned he did not notice that Chou had slipped his dagger from his scabbard so that when he reached for it, it was no longer there. He went to loosen the cudgel that swung from his waist, but as he did so he felt a sharp jab in his hand delivered to him by Chou with his own dagger.

'Agh,' he gasped, sucking his bleeding hand as Chou slipped behind him and cut the belt holding his cudgel. It fell to the ground and Chou scooped it up before he had time to take in what had happened. Neither of the other two brigands saw any of this as it was taking place behind them and to their left, but Ryo saw it all from where he stood, squaring up to the mean, lean brigand.

The big one stepped back from Daiki who still held his sword, which had far greater reach than the dagger in his hand. The big brigand was aware now that the odds were at least even, since neither he nor the lean one had their swords. Instinctively he stepped back to where he assumed the stout man to be, who would hopefully cover his back. He did not know that Chou was already dealing with him. Only Ryo and the villagers saw her next move. She dropped to the ground, picked up the cudgel, delivered a smart blow to the stout man's foot and as he lifted it in pain she rose quickly and pushed him. As he went down heavily she took one pace forward and jabbed the big one in the bottom with the narrow end of the cudgel. He swivelled round in response and as he did so she hit his dagger hand with the cudgel. He made an angry grunt and dropped the dagger. With her lightning speed Chou had the dagger in her hand and had drawn back to a safe distance. She saw the stout man recovering himself and reaching for his own dagger which Chou had left on the ground in order to pick up the cudgel. She hurled the cudgel through the air and it hit his hand as it reached for the dagger and again he recoiled in pain, holding his damaged hand.

All four of the young companions could now read the situation clearly. Only the lean man had a weapon in his grasp, and just a dagger at that. The brigands' other weapons were now out of their reach as Chou had pounced on the stout man's dagger as he withdrew to nurse his hand.

Ryo noticed that the cudgel had come to rest just behind the big brigand's right foot. To Ryo's right was Daiki, holding the brigand's sword and thus stopping him from advancing. Chou was behind the brigand, a little further back, standing over the stout man who was sitting on the ground and still holding his damaged hand. She was holding his dagger menacingly towards him and by now he realized how swift and sharp she was so was staying still.

Seizing his opportunity Ryo lunged towards the big brigand with his spear, as if intending to jab him in the chest. It had the desired effect. He stepped back and stumbled on the cudgel and as he lost his balance Daiki also rushed forward and pushed him hard. Daiki's weight and force sent him crashing down. Daiki stepped forward and stood above him with the sword at the ready. The man stayed down, breathing heavily and in pain.

Ryo had returned his attention to the lean man who he assumed still to have his dagger in his left hand. He would still be a danger. But as Ryo had jabbed at the big one, the lean one had lunged at him, giving Katsuo the opportunity for a decisive move. Katsuo had struck at his knife hand with the blade of the hoe, dislodging the knife, which fell to the ground. This was Katsuo's moment. He swept at the man's legs with the blade, but this brigand was agile, as Daiki had guessed. He leaped above the hoe with speed and exactness, landing to face Katsuo in unarmed combat mode. Without hesitation Katsuo tossed the hoe aside and prepared for one-to-one combat, without weapons.

Ryo came in on this with his spear at the ready.

But Katsuo hissed, 'Just back me up. This one is mine. He is unarmed now.'

Ryo stood by with spear held firm in case Katsuo was bettered by his opponent. He sensed how important this was for Katsuo, a first opportunity to test his finely tuned skills in authentic combat. So he did as asked, while tensed on full alert.

The lean brigand flew towards Katsuo with a barrage of swift, deadly punches to the head. But none of them landed. Katsuo dropped low and swept the man off his feet by rolling into his ankles. The man recovered himself and turned again in attack, but Katsuo was up and ready. Months of sparring practice were paying off. The brigand could see this youngster was highly skilled and very fit. Ryo could read that he knew he was well matched. As if putting all his energies into one last barrage the brigand went at Katsuo with a flying leap. For a split second Ryo thought he was going to impact Katsuo's chest with what would have been incapacitating force. But at the last moment Katsuo swivelled so that the brigand met nothing to stop him and flew through the air to crash into the bench. Tools scattered and the man collapsed onto the ground at which point Katsuo cried out to Ryo, 'Spear, now! Stand over him to prevent him from rising.'

Ryo was already halfway there, having sized things up for himself. Katsuo swept round in a circle to assess the whole situation. Once he had established that the other two were well guarded by Daiki and Chou, he looked at Ryo and smiled. 'Thanks for back-up,' he said quietly. 'And for letting me prove myself too.'

Ryo glanced up momentarily to see this but swept his gaze immediately back down to the brigand he was now guarding. This one was swift as a snake and needed watching carefully. Though by now it seemed unlikely he would try his luck again with four opponents to deal with, and each one evidently skilled in distinct ways.

'We must have them tied,' said Chou. 'Are the villagers ready with the rope?'

Chou had earlier arranged for several villagers to have rope ready to truss up the brigands once they had been overcome. That way they could then be delivered by cart to the marshal's care. From there they would be tried and dealt with according to the law.

The four companions stood over the brigands as pairs of villagers came forward to tie them securely. Once tied and hobbled so they could use neither hands nor feet they were jostled and loaded onto a wagon and then tied in place on the wagon itself. The companions were leaving it to the villagers to deliver the brigands into the hands of the law. They could not afford to do this themselves as it would have drawn attention to their status as Hidden Ones, which was obviously to be avoided as much as possible.

With the advice of the village head elder they chose suitable villagers to accomplish this task, ones capable of keeping an alert eye on the brigands and of managing the brigands' weapons to control them, should they manage to untie themselves.

Eventually the four companions had the satisfaction of seeing the wagon, pulled by two bullocks, creak its way out of the village on the long journey to the district marshal. As it left Ryo noticed Azami standing in the doorway of a nearby hut. From that place she had watched the entire proceedings and had at no point needed to consider entering the fray. The mission had, at the least, been a success. The task had been accomplished. Azami would probably take them through the event again, analysing who had done what along with the other options they might have taken. At many moments in a fight split-second decisions are taken which will have a knock-on effect as things proceed. And where three adversaries are met by four the variables are multiplied. It is a subtle mix of planning and opportunism with many points where chance intervenes. The more skill and experience a fighter has, the more chance is reduced. But chance can never be eradicated entirely.

The villagers and the village elders were delighted with the outcome. They thanked the four companions profusely. Daiki beamed with pleasure throughout. Chou smiled and nodded with gracious modesty. Katsuo nodded and bowed with stiff formality. And Ryo flushed and said, 'Really, I just helped and backed up. It was the others that did the main work.'

But when Azami heard him say that she noted it. She had marked how throughout the proceedings Ryo had had a clear command of what was going on with each party. He had only moved and acted when it was necessary and all of his moves, though slight, had been intelligently measured and judged. She knew that he had been an essential part of the process and had blended effectively with the varied yet combined skills of the other three. She resolved to tell him this later at an opportune moment.

The village elders served them tea with rice cakes to thank them for their assistance. This was served out of doors in the compound. When this was over and it was time to leave, the villagers lined up, forming an avenue for them to walk through. As they did so the villagers bowed and thanked them as they passed. Soon they were back on the track that left the village, making their way swiftly and silently towards their own home at the Hill Camp.

Time passed and Ryo was getting back into the rhythm of life at the Hill Camp. Some days he was tending the animals. Some days he was hoeing and weeding the vegetables. And some days he was practising hard, either alone, or at the main sessions with the teachers. And he was continuing to spar playfully with his three companions back at their compound. He was still no real match for any of them, but they treated him like a younger brother in respect of his fighting. And he was growing gradually better at reading their styles and predicting their moves, even though he was not yet swift or skilled enough to prevent them in time. Though just occasionally he would catch one of them off their guard and manage to topple them.

It was at this point that the idea of the Great Change was introduced. Everyone in the camp was called to a full meeting in the Main Hall. Akio was there on the dais, sitting quietly while people filed in to sit on the floor. Ryo caught himself thinking what a mass of skill and talent was closely collected in one place. Knowing the abilities of many there he thought what a formidable body they made.

Akio rang the gong, which signalled the beginning of his address. Everyone listened attentively. Such an event was rare so this must be a matter of importance.

'Our tradition, as all of you know,' he began, 'goes back several centuries. The fighting arts we cultivate here were once taught in many places. It was Unzen who brought them together to establish the Hill Camp some forty years ago. He gathered together the best of practices and distilled them to create what we teach and learn here. And we have continued to develop them. Unzen, as you know, due to his age, retired to the traditional life of the hermit, leaving me, Akio, to take his place as your leader. It is as your leader that I now address you.' He paused for a moment to scan the many faces in front of him. They were silent, attentive and expectant.

'Until now we have maintained a jealous independence from the world we live in. Occasionally we have intervened when necessary. Particularly when extreme injustices needed to be challenged. But mostly we have kept to ourselves, even to the point of self-sufficiency in material ways. The outside world has up till now been politically unreliable. Clans have feuded with clans. Warlords have tussled with each other over territory and assets. Ours has been a land of pirates and robber barons, and in wilder places brigands have roamed unchecked, unless they've made the mistake of coming our way.' He smiled quietly at his last remark and there was a ripple of amusement from his audience.

Ryo cocked his head to listen carefully. Akio was clearly on the verge of announcing something of great significance.

'But all this is changing. For several years now Emperor Hayato, The Falcon, has been bringing a nation together out of all this chaos. He has amassed a powerful army and has subjugated the strongest warlords in the country through his strength and cunning. He seeks to establish a land of peace and stability where honest folk can go about their business unmolested, where trade can flourish and where culture can thrive. Perhaps soon ordinary people may sleep more peacefully in their beds at night.

'All this is good, of course. But it affects our position in the Hill Camp here. Were we to remain something of a legend as to our existence and whereabouts, it would be only a matter of time before Hayato would wish to send out scouts in search of us. To have a force like us at large in a settled state might understandably fill a ruler with unease. To him we may seem no better than the many bands of brigands that have abounded up until now.

'It was with this in mind that not long ago I sought an audience with him and negotiated terms for inclusion in his plans. The Hidden People will no longer be hidden in the New Empire. This will be a great change for us, but it is unavoidable. As we always say, everything changes and we must allow change to flow through us as it does with all things. Nothing can stay the same for ever and we must now move with the times.

'Emperor Hayato wishes to witness our skill and power. He wishes us to remain as a force he can call on to maintain civil order in the New Empire. And he also wishes us to be available as a military unit should serious defence measures be required. To that end most of us will soon make the journey to his capital in order to engage in a mass demonstration of all that we can do. He wants to see how equipped we might be to serve him.

'A few of us must remain behind to maintain the Hill Camp in our absence. I will appoint a mixture of the oldest members and the very youngest to do this. It's possible that the Hill Camp may remain as our home and our base in the future. But it is also possible we may be required to close it down in order to remove ourselves nearer to the capital where Hayato has his stronghold. This will be decided in time.

'For now, though, we have a journey to prepare for. We'll travel lightly, as we always do. I've already discussed this with key teachers and they will pass on what's required of you in fuller detail. I will be travelling with you, of course. So I'll see you on the journey. Be prepared, be attentive, be vigilant. That is all.'

Akio sounded the gong whose deep boom reverberated around an otherwise silent hall. For a moment, as its echoes died away, everyone was still as silence settled back over the room. Then people started to move quietly and thoughtfully out of the hall to return to their compounds.

But what of me? thought Ryo as he walked back to his compound with his three companions. Will I be included in the journey? Or will I be left here to tend the crops and animals, along with those now too old or too young to take part?

His questions were soon answered. His counsellor informed him that he was a special case. He was now considered to be experienced enough to go on the journey. But as he was not sufficiently fledged as a fighter to be part of the force, Akio wanted him to go along as a scout. At times he would travel with the group. But sometimes he would be sent out to scan the landscape for signs of movement and activity. Eventually the group would be met by one of the Emperor's military units who would accompany Akio's force into the capital.

Well, thought Ryo, at least I'm considered worthy of going along for the ride. That's better than nothing. Better, I reckon, than staying here to mind the farm. At least they're taking me seriously now.

Chapter Thirteen

Three days on from Akio's address to the company they were ready to leave. They set off early in the morning, in a grey light streaked with wispy mist. Everyone carried a sparse bundle, much as Unzen and Ryo had on their journey from Cold Mountain to the Hill Camp. The idea was to move swiftly through the landscape and to camp minimally each night with just a small sleeping sack and modest rations. In this way they would demonstrate how effective they might be as a light unit with the ability to travel at speed and attracting minimum notice. One of the essential virtues of the Hidden Ones was their ability to impact lightly on the world and yet to wield great force with little display. For that reason they observed the discipline of travelling in silence. Nobody chattered. Only essential words were used for practical purposes, and these were uttered briefly and quietly. Part of their training had been to develop an aptitude for stillness and silence when words and movement were inessential. So all members had acquired great discipline in this respect. As Ryo travelled with them he marvelled at their sure, steady efficiency. This helped him to maintain his edge alongside them, and so to feel that he belonged.

From time to time he was sent up to the side of the group, particularly when there were rises in the land from which the further landscape could be surveyed. On his return he would report to Akio to tell him what he'd seen. On one occasion he spotted a band of soldiers. Their armour and weapons glinted in the sun, and as the breeze shifted he could just hear the faint jingling of the horses' bridles and the clatter of their equipment.

How different, thought Ryo, from our way. They declare themselves from a distance, as if to say, 'Keep out of our way. We are coming. Or if you want combat, stay right there in our path . . .' Whereas we cut a silent swathe through the world, barely rustling the grass.

When he mentioned the soldiers to Akio, Akio just nodded once.

'Not our problem,' he said quietly. 'If they come our way we will melt away and let them pass. They won't have any idea of our presence as they go by.'

But as Akio had surmised from Ryo's report, they came nowhere near and posed no problem to the company. They were travelling in the opposite direction to the Hidden Ones.

So the journey proceeded smoothly. It was to take several days. On the morning of the last day Ryo found himself in a state of nervous but eager anticipation. His fellows showed no evidence of sharing his feelings. There was no way of telling whether they too had such emotions but were well enough disciplined to contain them. But he put it down to his own lack of experience and development. He was excited by the prospect of seeing, for the first time in his life, a great city. He'd only ever known villages, Cold Mountain and the Hill Camp. He'd never seen a large building made of stone, such as Daiki and Chou had mentioned during talks around the compound fire. 'A building of stone,' he'd marvelled. 'What must that be like?'

That last day of the journey passed peaceably enough. The company knew that later in the day they would be met by the Emperor's men in order to be led into the capital. Akio would be briefed by the reception party about what to expect before the whole retinue made their way into the city.

Late in the afternoon they entered a valley and Ryo, according to his standard instructions, made his way up to the right of the company, swiftly climbing the slope so as to be able to see beyond the valley to whatever might lie outside. As he came to the top of the rise he let out a gasp. He had never seen such a fine sight. It must be Emperor Hayato's capital! It was like a hundred, no, a thousand villages sewn together in a vast tapestry. And yet it was more than that. For at the centre were several large buildings, some made of stone and others built of wood and with orange tiled roofs and great pillars hewn from trees, the size of which Ryo had never seen. One or two buildings were like towers that reached into the sky, layer on layer. How dizzying to climb such a tower and look out from the top.

Do people really live in such a place? mused Ryo. What must it be like to make one's home among so many buildings and so many people? How strange.

But Ryo had a job to do. He took control of himself and contained his excitement about the city. He began to scan the landscape, starting with the far and moving his gaze in towards the near. As he shifted his attention to the valley itself he saw that at the far end there was a large band of soldiers, many on horseback and still more holding spears. They were all helmeted and armoured and were silent and waiting. A commander on a fine horse sat mounted at their head. They must be the reception party, ready to lead Akio's people into the city. How impressive they looked, compared to the Hidden Ones in their simple, plain clothes with their small bundles and wooden staves. But Ryo, of course, reflected on how, should it come to such a thing, his people could probably unhorse in no time those pompous soldiers and have the spears out of the foot soldiers' hands as easily.

As he watched and waited, preparing himself for the descent to rejoin his people, a strange thing happened which held him back. What was this? The Hidden Ones were all falling to the ground! What were they doing? Was this some kind of strange display prepared for the reception party? What could it mean? As Ryo screwed up his eyes to see more distinctly he could see arms stirring and legs twitching, as if his company had been struck down by some strange malady, some rapid sickness which had passed over them all like a wave.

And then he saw the foot soldiers advancing, unchecked, with spears at the ready, moving amongst his fallen companions, stabbing and thrusting at them as if to finish the business of whatever had struck them down in the first place. What had happened? How could they all have fallen so swiftly? What could possibly have struck them down? Was this really a massacre? Was it really happening? Or was this some kind of strange exercise, an enactment of some kind that Ryo had not been made aware of?

But now Ryo noticed something else happening. On the far side of the valley there was movement on the hillside. Figures seemed to be emerging from the earth itself. As he strained his eyes again to peer he realized they must have been concealed in holes dug into the valley sides. And they were all carrying something, the like of which he'd never seen. He knew what a bow looked like. And his first thought was that these were archers, hidden to fire from the secrecy of their individual holes. But these were not bows. Or if they were, they were bows like none Ryo had ever seen. Whatever these weapons were they were swift, deadly, silent and sure. And fired from secrecy as they had been, there had been no hint Ryo's companions could possibly have picked up on. They had been struck down ruthlessly with no warning signs that they were under attack. Against this onslaught all their fine defensive skills had been as nought.

Once the concealed figures had emerged from the far hillside and the foot soldiers showed signs of completing their grisly business among the fallen company, the full impact of what had happened began to flood into Ryo's mind. His comrades had been slain quite suddenly out of the blue.

What he first felt was confusion. And quickly on the heels of that, horror. For now, his mind was in a whirl. So much so that he was rooted to the spot, unable to move, uncertain of what direction to take, of what, simply, to do with himself. His training began to kick in, however, and his next impulse was to hide himself in case there were further concealed assassins on his side of the valley. The first thing was to make sure he stayed alive. After that he would decide what he might do next. The chances of any of the company below surviving were not worth considering, so thorough had been the nature of the massacre, planned and executed with cruel and exact precision.

So he climbed a tree that had foliage dense enough to screen him from ground-level sight and prepared for time to pass and things to settle.

As he sat in the tree he began to collect his thoughts. To begin with, though, he needed to calm himself. He could feel his blood pounding, his heart and his head throbbing. So for a short while he shut his eyes and breathed consciously into his abdomen, allowing the breath to settle there briefly before breathing out again through his mouth. For several minutes he persisted with this until he felt steadier. When this was the case he began to allow his mind to play over the events that had so recently taken place . . .

Clearly, there had been an ambush. This had been planned well in advance, and since his whole company had been massacred then this had long been intended. The whole agreement with the Emperor must have been a hoax, a trick, to lure the Hidden Ones from their wasteland lair in order to wipe them out. Ryo could only surmise that the Emperor must have considered them a risk to state security, too much a maverick or outlaw organization to be trusted. Too skilled and dangerous a body to have in one's army, like a savage dog that might turn on its owner. But if this was the case how wrong he had been. If only he had been prepared to study their ways and consider their ideas and principles. If he'd come to understand the culture of the Hidden People he would never have thought it necessary to destroy them.

Such thoughts swirled through Ryo's mind as he sat in the tree and the day passed. He stayed quiet and still, intending to wait until the light was fading so that he might cover some ground under cover of darkness. His immediate plan was to return to the Hill Camp to warn those left there of what had happened. His main concern at present was simply to stay alive and to make that journey. Before long a strange sickly sweet smell began to come to him on the light afternoon breeze. What was this? From his vantage point he could just see down into the valley. Smoke was rising. Oh, he thought with a sense of pain, they are burning the bodies. Of course . . .

He visualized Akio, that calm, steady being with such dignity and skill, dead now and succumbing to the flames. And then he thought of Chou, Daiki and Katsuo, who had all been accepted into the company for the journey. His friends, his companions, almost his family, it had begun to seem. They were so young. They had so much time and promise ahead of them. Yet now it had all been snatched away in a matter of moments. And he, Ryo, why had he been spared? Well, that was chance, simply. Because he was a scout he had not been with them when the mystery arrows had been shot. It was as arbitrary, as meaningless, as that. He did not think himself lucky at this time. He felt, rather, that he ought to be dead with his fellows. By what right was he alive and they dead? What was so special about him, compared to so many of them who were so much further trained and more finely skilled? It was stupid. Chance, or fate, or whatever you might call it, was a stupid, brainless agency, indiscriminate in its actions. Why should good people die at the hands of those with less skill, less understanding, less moral sense than them? Ryo could not accept it. And yet he could not deny it. It had happened. There was nothing he could do to undo it. Still so fresh, it was already in the past, a done deed.

Suddenly Ryo felt a surge of rage, a wild, red anger, rush through him. Momentarily it took over his whole being, so that his impotence, his inability to do anything to change things, tipped him towards a furious scream. Again, his training came to his rescue. A scream so loud might be heard and bring soldiers running his way. He must acknowledge yet direct his rage and bring it to stillness. The rage was there, yes, it could not be denied. But he must not allow it to betray his presence, for this would put him into the hands of his adversaries and he would lose the slender power to act that he still held. Ryo clenched his teeth, grimaced and squeezed the tree branch until his knuckles turned white. Inwardly he raged and screamed but no sound emerged from him to give his presence away. Gradually the rage subsided, leaving him feeling drained and empty. Now he had to wait quietly until it seemed safe to make his escape from the vicinity.

When the day had advanced enough and the light was beginning to fade, Ryo listened out carefully for any sound of movement in his immediate surroundings. Unzen had trained him well in this respect so he could distinguish sounds of breeze or woodland creatures from any probable hints of human presence. He ate a little rice cake and dried plum and drank some water from his flask to give him energy for his journey. Then, slipping down from the tree, he slung his bundle over his shoulder and started back towards the Hill Camp.

His plan was to stay on the high ground as much as possible, while trailing the journey they had come, tracing it backwards. Since he had scouted for the group he had a good grasp of the route. As he came to places he recognized he could recall the ways they had come by. It would be simply a matter of making the journey and catching sleep in short bouts in order to preserve his best energies in case they might be needed.

He didn't travel far that first night. He managed to remove himself from the area of the massacre, which was his first purpose. That way he would be further from the city and further from the killing ground where the Emperor's soldiers might still be engaged in clearing-up procedures, burning and burial, removal of the carnage. Once he deemed himself sufficiently far enough away from all of that, he took out his blanket from his bundle, found a dry, safe place to sleep, gathered some grass and bracken for warmth around him and fell asleep.

He woke in darkness with a slight start. Where was he? His exhaustion from the day before had made him sleep deeply, densely, so that it took him a moment before the events of yesterday came back to him. He felt a kind of creeping dread come over him, a kind of despair. It sapped him of energy so that he did not want to move. He just wanted to stay there in his blanket in the darkness and give up. Perhaps if he lay there long enough he would die and the creatures of the wild would gradually dismember his body and leave his bones to decay into the soil with the help of wind and weather. Then it would be over, all this effort and pain and misery. But he remembered what Unzen had taught him and he lay and watched his breath entering and leaving his body. He practised the art of looking with kindness, with compassion, at first his bodily sensations, then his emotions and in due course his thoughts. And then he drew back from those experiences and simply watched them with kind curiosity while continuing to breathe and to be aware of that breathing which automatically kept him alive. His companions were dead. He was alive. He was separated from them for ever in this life. And he had at least one job still to do, to visit the Hill Camp to take the sad news to the few that remained there. He did not relish the task. But he knew it was his duty. Akio and Unzen would have said so, he was sure. So for now it provided a purpose, a reason to carry on. It was something to do.

The return to the Hill Camp was uneventful, though Ryo's mind was kept very busy throughout the journey. It kept playing back over all that had taken place since Unzen had left him at the camp to begin his training. Events, scenes, relationships, interviews, all of it, it swirled into and around his mind before passing out again to be replaced by some other associated memory.

Once, just once, Ryo saw a solitary woodman down below. Beside him was a mule carrying a load of firewood. They were so distant that they looked like little ants making their way along the narrow trail into the mountains, a direction that Ryo would not be taking. It reminded Ryo of an image which his father sometimes painted on his vases before firing them. 'The solitary woodman wending his way.' His father had once explained that this figure represented the journey we all make through life. He stood for the way we at times seem to toil on an upward journey, alone. The comfort it might bring, his father had said, is that we can consider that it's the same for all of us. Each single one of us must make that slow, solitary journey. And we can tell ourselves that somewhere ahead of him, hidden in the mountains, is a small hut where tea and rice and rest await him, and perhaps even the company of a wife and children or at least some kind of comradeship. Seeing the woodman there gave Ryo a little grain of hope that all might not be lost. Perhaps he could salvage something out of all that had taken place for him. Who could say what the future might hold if he could only just keep going for now? He must be like that woodman and simply wend his way, step by step, breath by breath.

CHAPTER FOURTEEN

At last the Hill Camp was within sight. As he approached Ryo began to plan his words. He would need to gather everyone there together and then give them a sensible account of what had taken place. He must prepare for their shock, their horror, their grief and their reactions to the massacre of their comrades and friends. It would not be easy. And he would have to contain his own grief in order to give a clear account. To put in to words for others what he had hardly come to terms with himself would be a trial and a challenge. But he must prepare to do his best.

The ascent to the gate at the upper rim was as arduous as Ryo remembered. When he had first made the climb it had been laced with a sense of hope and expectation. Excitement had fed energy into his blood. Now it was a weary climb, heavy hearted and slow footed. But he made his way to the top, doggedly, thinking through his prepared speech to those waiting there. It was quiet, but then most of the company was no longer there, just a few older and younger members to keep the camp in good order against the eventual return of their comrades.

As Ryo passed through the entrance he was surprised to find no one there to challenge him. Why was there nobody on guard at the gateway? Puzzled, he went on in, a little cautiously at first. And then he saw. His stomach seemed to fall away inside him and he heard himself let out a gasp of shock.

The camp had been destroyed. The main halls had been burned down and there was disarray everywhere. There was no sign of the members who had been left behind to maintain the camp and the animals were gone too.

Ryo felt sick and giddy. This must really be the end. Now there seemed nothing at all left. Everything in his life had been swept away. He sat down on the ground with his head in his hands and moaned. And then he lost consciousness. The events of the last few days had taken their toll. He had eaten little and walked hard and in high alertness and slept lightly while travelling. His body was worn down and his emotions had taken a beating. This last blow was too much.

After a while he came to, feeling dazed. In a

light-headed, numb state, he decided to walk through the camp. There might be some food somewhere. Perhaps he could eat something and find somewhere to rest properly while deciding what to do next, where to go. For now his future lay blank in front of him, though that was masked by his need simply to stay alive from hour to hour. He had no sense of being in imminent danger. The camp had been sacked. Whoever had done it had been and gone. There would be no point now, surely, in their returning here? So for now, for the purpose of getting rest and food, he should be safe for a day or so if necessary.

He went, more from force of habit than for any other reason, to the hut compound he'd shared with Daiki, Katsuo and Chou. They had a wooden box where they kept rice and lentils and dried beans. He'd often cooked simple meals on the fire outside their hut so he planned to do just that once more, before making a safe, dry bed in which to get some good rest. He knew the importance of looking after the body's basic needs under conditions of great pressure. He must stay well and strong in order to survive his present ordeal.

He found what he needed and went through the motions of making his meal. It was a sad business, as it brought back memories of cooking with his companions there while they all chatted together about their lives, their past experiences and their thoughts about the future. Now Ryo only had his own life and thoughts to reflect on and they seemed very dismal in a world that was shared with no one.

He sat watching the beans simmer in the small iron pot that hung above the fire. Whoever had sacked the camp had come to close it down and remove the people and animals. They had not been interested in stealing things from the smaller huts so this suggested to Ryo that it might have been part of the plan to exterminate the Hidden Ones, part of the Emperor's plan. He recalled the troop of soldiers he'd seen riding in the opposite direction to the Hidden Ones, on a different route. Perhaps they had been on their way to the Hill Camp to rid it of surviving members. That would all fit . . .

As he was thinking these thoughts he sensed a slight movement out at the perimeter of the light thrown by his fire. The dusk had given way to darkness so he had to strain his eyes to peer at the source of the sound.

Then a small voice said tentatively, incredulously, 'Ryo . . . ? Surely not . . . ? Ryo . . . ?'

Ryo took in the slight, girlish shape approaching him slowly and with caution. Was this a ghost? It looked like . . . but no, could it be . . . ?

'Chou . . . ?' he heard himself utter in disbelief. 'Chou . . . ?'

But the small shape was rushing towards him and as

he rose in shock she flung herself at him and wrapped her arms around him tightly. As she did so she burst into a sobbing so intense Ryo could feel her small, bird-like body throbbing against him. Something cracked inside him and his withheld grief also broke into deep sobs that seemed to wrack his whole body. For a while they clung together, their griefs seeming to interfuse, their tears soaking into each other's hair and clothes.

And then they parted slightly, still holding on to one another, looking intensely at each other, and patting each other to convince themselves of their very substance, to reassure themselves that they were not ghosts, not visions, but real living beings.

'I thought you were dead. I thought I was the only one left,' babbled Ryo. 'I thought there was just me—'

'I too,' Chou cut in. 'I thought the same.'

'But how did you survive?' asked Ryo in amazement. 'I was up the side of the valley, scouting. But surely you were with the others? How did the soldiers miss you? How did you escape the magic arrows?'

'I was scouting that time, like you,' said Chou. 'Akio told me to go up the opposite side of the valley, to make sure all seemed safe. So I was up there when the bowmen fired their volleys. I was just above them, luckily. I might have stumbled upon them, they were so well concealed. But I had climbed high, so the highest boltholes they were hidden in were just below me. When they'd fired their arrows and our comrades had fallen, they began to emerge from their holes, like foxes. Of course, I kept myself well concealed so they did not notice me. But I saw them clearly. They must have been the Emperor's men. They were carrying strange mechanical bows, the like of which I've never seen. They fire metal arrows silently, like a deadly rain when there are many, like then.'

'Yes,' said Ryo. 'I saw them emerge from their holes, also, from across the valley. But I could not see their weapons from that distance. I returned to the Hill Camp to warn the people here of what had happened. Only to find what you must have seen for yourself too.'

'Yes,' said Chou sadly. 'It has all been ended. All wiped away. I cannot say why the Emperor would do such a thing. Why would he want to? Surely we could have been of such use to him? It makes no sense.'

Ryo explained the thoughts he'd had while hiding up the tree before his journey back to the Hill Camp. As he spelled out what he'd guessed Chou sat listening thoughtfully, nodding at his words.

'Yes,' she said. 'That must be it. It could be so. It is the only explanation.' Then she said suddenly, 'Ryo, what are you going to do now? Have you thought about that yet?'

'There's food here,' said Ryo. 'I was going to eat

first, then get some good rest. Then I was going to work out what to do after that. Eat some food. You must be tired and hungry. You've been travelling like me. Share the food then get some rest in the hut with me. Food, warmth and sleep. And then we can work out what to do with ourselves. Does that make sense?'

Chou nodded. Together they sat by the fire, eating the rice and beans from rough wooden bowls and drinking wheat tea that Ryo had brewed while cooking. They ate and drank in silence, both brooding on all that had happened and taking stock of their situation and the decisions to be made.

Before they retired Chou spoke. As she did so she did not look at Ryo, but stared into the embers of the dying fire.

'I think I know what I'm going to do next,' she said decisively. 'I am going to visit my village of origin.'

Ryo noted that she did not say 'my family'. Perhaps this was out of caution. There might be none of from family surviving by now. Times were hard for peasants back then. They might have died in a famine, or from plague or pestilence. It was prudent of Chou not to assume she had surviving family. But then Ryo remembered her story. As an unwelcome girl child she had been left out on a hillside to die. Her return might be considered bad luck. So perhaps she was going out of curiosity, simply to see what she might find there, and to discover what she could about her original roots.

'Will you stay there?' asked Ryo. 'Will you seek to settle there?' he pressed.

'No,' said Chou. 'They would not want me and I would not wish it. Imagine even if I did find my family and they agreed to take me in. Their guilt towards me would make them come to resent me, even if I did manage to forgive them myself. Things would grow sour and I would soon need to be gone. I simply want to see where I came from. And then move on.'

'But where?' Ryo persisted.

'I might try my luck in the city, at the Capital. The glimpse I got just before the massacre made me think that I might find work there. A girl like me, young and strong, could probably find employment. It would be some kind of a life. Who knows what might offer itself in due course?'

'You could go to my village,' Ryo offered tentatively. 'My family would take you in, I know, if you explained your relation to me. They would let you stay there. My mother would be glad of the help you would give her. And I know my younger sister, Hana, would love you. I can tell,' he said looking at her. He imagined the two of them together and it felt right. For a moment the image soothed him. But then Chou cut back in.

'And what of you, Ryo? What will you do? Where will you go next?'

Ryo answered swiftly. He had made up his mind while eating and staring into the fire. 'I want to go back and find Unzen. It's my duty, I think. I must tell him about what has happened. And then I'll ask his advice. He may not tell me, but he will help me decide. He has a knack for such things. Talking to Unzen usually helps to open a good trail.'

Chou nodded. 'I'm tired now, Ryo,' she said. 'Let's sleep. We need good rest before our journeys. We both have roads to travel tomorrow.'

Ryo and Chou made up their beds in the small hut. Then the two companions bade each other goodnight. Tonight they should be able to sleep in safety. Tomorrow they would go their separate ways.

Chapter Fifteen

Ryo and Chou rose quietly the next day. They spoke little but concentrated on equipping themselves for their journeys. They made rice balls and found dried provisions that would carry easily in their bundles. They each took a staff which, while appearing as a traveller's stick, could in their trained hands become a formidable weapon. They had each spent many hours practising the art of stave-fighting, so it would afford them some protection on the road in the event of hostile encounters. By the time they were ready to leave they looked like pilgrims or wandering monks, in their humble brown robes with their sticks and their bundles.

They left the Hill Camp together by the gate on the rim. They paused before leaving to look back over the camp one more time. It was a sorry sight. The main halls had been destroyed by fire. Empty of people and life it was a ghost of its former self. It was clear they were both saying their goodbye to it. They would probably never return here again. Gradually nature would take over and the camp would eventually be reclaimed by wild grasses. It was already falling away into the past and becoming history. They turned quietly and descended the steep path to the bottom of the hill.

At the foot of the hill Ryo repeated his offer to Chou. 'Remember,' he said. 'My home is at Furukawa, the village of the Old River. My father is the potter there. But even my name, Ryo, will take you to my family home. You will be well received there if you state your connection to me. When you have finished investigating your own family past this could be somewhere for you to start out on life again. Perhaps when I have seen Unzen I will see you there. One day soon I must go back and visit. I have been too long away. But for now my duty is to find Unzen. I will start by returning to Cold Mountain. That is the first place to seek him.'

The two companions said their farewells and parted. To separate was difficult for them both, but by observing the formal code for saying goodbye they each managed to contain their emotions. Chou took the path that would lead towards her village of origin. Ryo set out on the journey to Cold Mountain and Unzen's hermitage.

As Ryo walked the path back to Cold Mountain he thought of the journey he'd made in the other direction, almost a year ago now, with Unzen. Then he'd been full of hope and expectation. Now he was uncertain. He was still struggling with feelings of horror and sadness at the massacre of his companions. But, as well as those immediate feelings, he had the sense that all he'd been planning his life around had been wiped away at one single stroke. Unzen had often said to him that nothing in life was certain, not even his own life and survival. To live each day, each moment, for that moment, was a good strategy, allowing for the fact that one should plan prudently for a future which might never come. Even Ryo's father, Takumi, back in the workshop in Furukawa, had said similar things to Ryo as he began to grow up.

About halfway along his journey to Cold Mountain Ryo had a curious encounter. Coming down the trail towards him was a small man dressed in shabby black robes and wearing a straw hat. This was the kind of hat peasants wore when working in the paddy fields, to keep off both sun and rain. He had a small bundle slung from his shoulder and carried a stick. Ryo could see him coming from a long way off, as at that point the trail was visible a long way ahead, winding upward from Ryo's point of view. Every so often the man would stop. Sometimes he would look into the middle distance, sometimes into the far. But at one point he squatted down on his haunches to peer at something apparently right in front of him on the path. It was as if he was constantly looking attentively at his surroundings, at whatever presented itself to him at the time. Sometimes he seemed paused in reflection, as if talking to himself. Ryo was struck by this odd behaviour and found himself wondering who this strange traveller might turn out to be.

In due course they were only yards apart. At this point the man stopped. Observing politeness Ryo also stopped. The man nodded to him and gave a small bow. Ryo returned the greeting. The man was quite old and wizened. He carried no spare flesh, to judge from his face. He clearly lived on little and spent much time on the move. But he did not seem tired or needy in any way. His eyes were bright and there was a sinewy wiriness about him, as if he lived on air and rain for much of the time.

'Greetings,' said the old man.

Ryo echoed the courtesy.

'I am Daremo, the poet,' he added by way of introduction.

'And I am Ryo, bound for Cold Mountain,' returned Ryo.

At the sound of Ryo's destination the old man's eyes lit up. 'Ah, Cold Mountain,' he exclaimed. 'Fine place. Place of great distinction. Once home to Kanzan, legendary poet now dead,' he sighed. Then, looking at Ryo, he asked, 'Why do you go there? What is your purpose?'

Ryo looked away across the ravine to where the mountains were wrapped in mist. 'I don't know,' said Ryo quite naturally, as if talking to this old man he could be entirely honest. 'Everything I had has been swept away. I no longer know my purpose . . .' He looked back at the old man who was peering intently into his face.

'Ah,' said Daremo with sympathy. 'And you so young. Life is not always kind. Let me make you a poem to take with you.'

This might have seemed odd to Ryo, but the old man said it with such ease, such naturalness, that he just nodded and waited. The old man gazed across towards the mountains and was clearly thinking, composing the words to the poem in his head. Ryo waited silently. Eventually the old man stood up solemnly and prepared to speak. His delivery was formal. His utterance was a kind of performance, like a song or a short speech. This is what Ryo heard:

'Behind me the narrow trail has fallen away,
eroded by rough weathers.
Before me my way is unclear, shrouded in thick
mist.
Therefore I pick my way steadily, step by step,
breath by breath, along the uncertainty of this
winding mountain path.'

Ryo listened quietly as the poem came to him. It was about now, about where he actually was right now in the present time and place. This path, this journey, this weather. And yet it was also about where his life was now, where he, Ryo, was, in his current predicament. At one level it was simple, the actual here and now of plain facts. Yet at another level it went deeper. It was about his life, his future, his uncertainties, along with the need to go on, the need to do something, just something.

'Thank you,' said Ryo. 'Could you say it again so I can commit it to memory?'

Daremo repeated the poem while Ryo listened carefully. Then Ryo repeated it back to Daremo who nodded, saying, 'Yes, that's it. You have it now. It is with you always.'

Ryo nodded.

'And now we must go our ways,' said Daremo. 'I hope the path behind you has not entirely fallen away, though. Else I shall be plunged into the abyss. I was hoping for a few more years yet. But what will be will be, I suppose.' He sighed and smiled at Ryo, then gave him a small bow which Ryo returned.

The two travellers then turned from each other and went their ways. As Ryo walked on he murmured the words of the poem to himself a few more times so that it would remain firmly in his memory. In those times not much was written down and people had a capacity for remembering such things as poems, songs and stories. When one travels light the mind can be a good storehouse.

Ryo made good time on his journey. As he'd calculated, he only had to sleep two nights out in the open. By now he was well practised in the art of creating a warm, dry space for sleeping out. He made his provisions last and often found fresh water near the path, as he had with Unzen when travelling the other way.

As he went he reflected on all that had happened to him since leaving home so long ago. And from time to time he recited the poem that Daremo had made for him. The day soon broke when he would arrive at Unzen's hermitage on Cold Mountain. Ryo found himself looking forward to seeing the old man's familiar face and to sitting by the fire with him, sipping tea and talking or just looking quietly into the flames together. But he dreaded having to tell Unzen the terrible news of what had happened to the Hidden Ones and the Hill Camp. So it was with mixed feelings he approached Unzen's retreat on Cold Mountain. He longed for the sense of familiarity, warmth and security. But he shied from the thought of bringing such bad news to the old man.

When he arrived it was quiet and orderly but there was no immediate sign of Unzen. It was with some relief that Ryo noted that all was tidy and correct as usual. So he did not fear that yet again a familiar place had been overrun by Hayato's soldiers. This was one place that would be hard to find, and, besides, it was the dwelling place of just one old hermit to the few who knew of it. All the same Ryo wondered where Unzen might have gone. Had he closed up the old place and left for some other dwelling now that Ryo was no longer with him? It was late in the old man's life. Perhaps Cold Mountain was becoming too bleak a place to live out one's later days?

Although there was no fire smoking in the usual place and the door to Unzen's hut was closed, Ryo thought to look there first. Perhaps the old man was ill or resting. No harm in looking. He knocked quietly on the door, out of respect. Then, hearing no answer from within he knocked louder, pausing to say, 'Unzen, are you there? It's me, Ryo. I've come from the Hill Camp. I bring news. May I enter?'

But there was no reply. So politely, cautiously, he creaked the door open and peered inside. Nobody. Nobody there. All looked neat and peaceful so Ryo walked in. He entered as if entering a high palace or temple, almost holding his breath. Unzen's simple room was as tidy as ever. His few things were all in place. It was then that Ryo saw it . . . the scroll. It was an open scroll, the kind that usually carries poems, epigraphs or ink-brush pictures. It was hanging in the *tokonoma*, the shrine space where Unzen kept a vase with a simple flower arrangement. At present the vase contained a humble piece of dried grass. But the scroll bore a message, written in calligraphy with brush and ink. Ryo read its plain, firm words carefully:

'If you seek Unzen climb higher. Find me on the High Peak where I will be waiting with further teaching.'

Surely the High Peak was an inhospitable place, thought Ryo to himself, far less welcoming than the hermitage here? Was Unzen performing some ceremony there? Was he on a solitary retreat, to meditate nearer the sky or some such thing? Was the message on the scroll addressed to Ryo himself? Or was it simply an open message to anyone who happened to come seeking Unzen? The calligraphy on the scroll was perfectly executed. It was the work of an accomplished brushworker. So it was intended to be read as a kind of poem or aphorism, a statement in plain language which might bear a deeper truth. Such things, such gestures, were common in the culture back then. They still occur nowadays, but less so in these modern times.

So Ryo, leaving speculation aside, set off to climb

the path to the High Peak to find Unzen and to solve the mystery of the message on the scroll. He was tired but restless. He had expected to find Unzen by now so was feeling thwarted. His body was weary. But his spirit would not give him peace until this last mission for now was fulfilled. He drank some water and ate a remaining rice ball. He sat for a few minutes, breathing with his eyes shut, looking inside himself and gathering the energy he would need for this last push to the peak. It would probably only take a few hours, but he was tired and weak from his journey from the Hill Camp and he had not expected this further stage of walking, let alone climbing.

He went back the way he had come, to the fork in the trail where Unzen had once pointed to the way that led to the High Peak. From there could be seen a distinct path to follow but it was steep in places. And elsewhere it was narrow and winding and skirted deep drops into chasms of giddying depth. At times Ryo paused to take breath. When he did so he found he could gaze over further peaks which lay partly shrouded in mist or cloud. Sometimes the clouds looked to him like dragons, the kind he had seen painted on vases or on scrolls in the alcoves in people's dwellings.

The Dragons of Air, thought Ryo. It's as Unzen said. Up on the High Peaks one may encounter the Dragons of Air. Perhaps he has gone up there to commune with them. Perhaps that is the further teaching he refers to. Perhaps he is seeking further wisdom to pass on . . .

As Ryo climbed he found it increasingly hard to breathe, or, at least, to get energy from his breath. Through his training he was skilled and sensitive in the art of breathing and in the knack of reading his own body and its energies and states. The air seemed rarer as he rose to greater heights, so that at times he felt himself becoming giddy and feared losing his sense of balance.

But at last he could see what looked like the summit ahead. Although it still seemed a fair distance, the fact that he could see it meant he could measure his energies in order to reach it without succumbing to exhaustion. He walked on, marking places ahead where he would pause for breath. In this way he broke up the last stretch of the journey into stages which he could tackle one by one. Eventually he reached the summit itself.

Once there he realized the summit consisted of a large expanse of open flat ground, strewn liberally with boulders and smaller rocks. There was an area in the middle of all this that seemed clearer. Almost like a kind of natural platform littered with debris and small stones. As he walked into this arena-like space his sandals crunched on brittle, friable matter and when he stopped to consider it he saw he was scrunching on bones. He guessed this might be a feeding ground for birds of prey. Perhaps eagles brought young goat kids or rabbits they'd plundered from the valleys below, to eat them in peace up here, to tear the flesh from the bones, leaving just the carcass for the scavengers, the crows and vultures, to pick clean.

He noticed ahead a movement of something black. Could that be Unzen? He almost called out to him, but before he could do so, the shape moved and rose into the air and Ryo realized at once that it was a vulture, rising momentarily and flapping its ragged, black wings as if to air them and free them of dust. Maybe he had disturbed it. Human presence up here would be rare, so it might have been made uneasy by his approach.

As he drew closer the vulture rose, then another with it. The pair flapped lazily until they were just far enough away to feel safe from Ryo. Then they perched on a rock where they sat lurking, as if waiting for him to leave so they could resume whatever business they were about there.

Ryo advanced to where the vultures had risen from, and then he saw. It was the remains of a human body. The vultures had been at work on it so there was little flesh left on the skeleton. Perhaps foxes or jackals too had visited, for some of the limbs had become dismembered. The clothes had been reduced to rags by the depredations of the carrion creatures but a little hair remained on the skull, forming a grisly tonsure. And then Ryo saw the staff on the ground nearby. It was Unzen's. For a moment there was just shock, followed by a wave of horror. Ryo had been expecting to encounter Unzen up here on the High Peak. But he had expected nothing like this. He struggled to equate the gross wreckage in front of him with the man he had come to admire and respect so much, the man whose living presence was so full of knowledge, skill and understanding. Even his features, his face, had been removed by the ravening creatures. For a moment Ryo felt impelled to rush at the vultures with his staff or to hurl stones at them. But he knew it was pointless. These creatures just followed their nature. And they would not have killed Unzen. Carrion creatures are not predators. They prey on the dead. Unzen had come up here to die, as he had once ventured to Ryo that he might. He had been at the end of his life and he would have known that. So he had made the journey up here, lain his body down or sat in meditation if he'd still had the strength and then allowed himself to fade away, taking no food or water and allowing the wind and the weathers to coax his spirit out of his body which he would then bequeath to the carrion undertakers to dispose of.

This, of course, thought Ryo, was Unzen's further and final teaching. This was the meaning behind the cryptic words on the scroll that he'd left in his alcove, possibly for Ryo himself to read. Ryo had been meant to follow him up here to say farewell and to receive this final lesson. Ryo thought back on the many times Unzen had commented on his age and his mortality. He had been a man at the end of his life, with more thoughts on dying with dignity than on living for further purposes. This was as it should have been, Ryo realized. And Unzen had behaved in accordance with his principles, looking at death directly and with steady acceptance.

But it was still hard for Ryo to equate the ragged remains in front of him with his vivid memory of the man who had taught him so much, talked and listened to him and shared so many days with him.

Is this what we come to? thought Ryo. Even the wisest and the greatest of us? The body is broken down and returned to the cycles of nature. What the carrion creatures leave is taken back into the earth by the forces of decay. And even the bones are eventually worn and crushed to dust to merge with the basic, material substance of the earth. If we have such a thing as a spirit, then what form could it take once the body has been dismantled? Where could it possibly reside? Does it become a dragon of the air, a kind of insubstantial cloud ghost that wafts through the ether? Or does our entire being, including our consciousness, simply melt back into the processes of decay to make way for the many new living forms, both animal and vegetable, that are continually arising and coming into being from the fertile emptiness that gives rise to all?

The image of Unzen's remains, these thoughts that swirled around his mind and his utter exhaustion from hard travelling and bitter grief, all of these things finally came together to form a whirlpool, a giddy vortex, into which Ryo was sucked. He fell to the ground and lost consciousness.

When he came to he was aware of a strange presence near to him. He had a sense of something large, something vast, breathing slowly and deeply. As he rose from his blackout and turned he was amazed to see an immense scaly creature crouched on the ground about twenty paces from him. It had furled wings of tough skin and its scales seemed to swirl with rainbow colours, like those of an exotic fish. Its taloned claws rested on the ground beneath its bulk. It had the appearance of an enormous flying serpent, though now it was at rest.

He knew at once what it was. Although he had never seen such a thing for real he recognized it as a dragon, a Dragon of Air, his thoughts told him with certainty. He had seen images of such creatures on vases and on scroll paintings. But he'd never been sure whether they were supposedly real or simply mythical. Now, this vast, breathing bulk before him, and the warmth of its breath as it exhaled, told him most firmly that this was indeed a real creature.

He waited to see what would happen. He was awe-struck by the strangeness and the wonder of this beast. Yet he was not afraid. It did not seem to threaten him. True, one would be mad to attack such a thing. But attack would not somehow occur to one as a consideration. In a sense the creature seemed to claim reverence for itself, not as a god, but rather as an amazing expression of nature, a kind of being distilled from the powers of the elements. A life force.

Apart from its breathing it made no sound. Its wings rippled lightly in the breeze, but it simply crouched there looking at him. As he looked back at it, seeing into the dark pools of its eyes, he could hear a voice in his head, or was it just a thought, telling him to approach it and to climb onto its back. Normally this would not seem a wise thing to do with such a beast. Yet now it seemed the most natural of things, and not unsafe or imprudent at all. And somehow he had no resistance to the idea in any case. His feet were carrying him towards the dragon and now he was scrambling up onto a natural saddle that was formed by a kink in its backbone below its long neck and just in front of the joints of its wings. There were little tufts of strong, wiry hair that sprouted from the base of its neck and it seemed natural to grasp onto these as one might grip the mane of a horse to maintain balance, so Ryo did just that. He did not question why he was doing this but it was clearly somehow intended. For, once he was seated, the dragon spread its great leathery wings, flapped them vigorously and rose into the air above the peak. As it did so Ryo let out a gasp of amazement and sheer thrill. For a moment his stomach seemed to drop away below him and he gripped the tufty sprouts of hair until his knuckles whitened. He also dug into the sides of the dragon with his knees to secure his seat. But he soon found that the fluent movement of the dragon's body seemed to accommodate him and mysteriously hold him in, almost as if he and the dragon became temporarily merged or melded together. He was riding the dragon. He was the dragon and the dragon was him. Rider and steed seemed one.

Together they rose to what for Ryo was an immense height. At first they passed through cloud until he could see what seemed a vast land entirely composed of the vaporous substance. It looked so solid that he felt he could have walked upon it. And there, too bright, too intense to look at directly, was the sun itself, lighting up the cloudscape and filling it with bright-nesses and shadows. And then the dragon plunged back through the clouds until Ryo could see the world he knew, but far, far below so that it looked huge yet tiny, like a scroll painting where individual things each seem to have their minute existence in the great panoply of being.

The dragon flew lower and Ryo sighed. There was his village right below and, look, who was that small person walking out of the village? It was him, Ryo. And there was his family at the door to their home, the pottery. They were waving to him and looked sad. But he was walking firmly out of the village with a resolute air, his bundle slung over his shoulder.

And now the dragon turned and Ryo saw himself on the road to Cold Mountain, still making his way into an uncertain future. And look, there was the house where the kind man had given him hospitality, expecting nothing in return save some conversation.

And now they were above the Hermitage on Cold Mountain. He could see Unzen training him, creeping up on him to deliver an unexpected blow from behind. The sight of Unzen filled him momentarily with joy and love for the old man who had taken such trouble over him. It was wonderful to see him so full of life and energy.

The dragon wheeled and Ryo could see the Hill Camp. Look, there were Daiki, Katsuo and Chou playing at knockout contest while Ryo watched them intently. He could see Chou doing her dancing magic which had both Daiki and Katsuo ultimately flummoxed. He could feel himself smiling at the sight of his dear friends together doing what they did so well.

The dragon moved on and then Ryo flinched to see the Hidden People making their way through the valley of death. He saw the metal arrows rushing towards them and he saw them all topple helplessly in that strange, eerie silence. He felt tears prick from his eyes and for a moment his vision was blurred. When he regained clarity he saw himself on the narrow road to Cold Mountain standing with Daremo, the poet, no doubt listening to the poem that had been made for him.

And now he could see the summit of Cold Mountain once more. There were the vultures, and there were the pitiful remains of Unzen's body. As they descended the vultures rose once more to keep a safe distance between the dragon and themselves. They clearly knew that respect was due to this great creature.

The dragon landed and Ryo, feeling exhilarated but dazed, slipped from its back and felt his feet firmly back on the ground for a few seconds. But then all went black and he could only hear the dragon's breathing. That was all there was for a while. The slow in and out of the dragon's deep breath. But no, surely it was his own breath he was hearing? Yes, he could feel his abdomen rising and falling in rhythm to the sound, to the sensation.

His eyelids flickered to let in a little hazy light. He was lying on the ground, in the dust, among the bones. He pressed his hands against the ground to try and raise himself but then he passed out again.

Eventually he came to consciousness. He was able to sit up and as he did so he noted the vultures loitering nearby, watching him. They had clearly sensed he was not yet dead so had not ventured to peck at him. As he stirred they moved further back, cautiously. Ryo looked about. He saw no dragon, nor any sign of one having been there. But there were Unzen's remains. Perhaps he had dreamed the dragon? But he had not dreamed the death of Unzen, his old teacher. That fact was firmly rooted in reality, if anything was.

He stood up solemnly and made a deep bow to Unzen's remains. He made no attempt to arrange or cover them, respecting Unzen's intention to leave his corpse for natural forces to dismantle. But he felt he should say something. Dazed as he was, delirious almost, from exhaustion and intense experience, he kept it simple.

'Goodbye, Unzen,' he said. 'Goodbye and thank you for your help, your teaching. I will do my best to honour your memory.' He gave one more small bow, turned, and then made his way down the mountain before cold and darkness came on with the night.

Chapter Sixteen

It was dark by the time Ryo arrived back at the Hermitage. He did not light a fire. He simply gathered as much warm bedding as he could find, made up the bed in his old hut and closed the door to keep out some of the night's cold. Then he wrapped himself up as securely as he could and fell into a deep, sound sleep. He roused slightly, out of habit, in the early dawn, but such was his exhaustion that he rolled over, gathered his bedding around himself tightly and drifted back into sleep.

It was light outside and the sun was up by the time he woke fully. He lay on his back, glad of the warmth of his bedding. He did not try to get up. There was no hurry and nowhere particular to go, nothing particular to do. From where he lay he could see a shaft of sunlight coming through a crack in the door. In its beam myriad motes of dust were lit up like tiny treasures or perhaps like minute, shining creatures. They swirled and floated in and out of the beam of light. He watched them aimlessly for a long time. The sight and the movement soothed his spirits, so he simply lay and gazed at them. He did not think about the events of the past few days. His mind was tired. He was worn out, through and through. He needed deep rest and a temporary forgetting of all that had happened in the vivid, recent past.

Eventually he rose. He went out and washed with water from the nearby stream. Then he made himself some food with rations from Unzen's hut, first making up a fire as he had done so many times before. The familiarity of the place and the set routines of fetching water, washing, lighting the fire and cooking, all those things soothed him and helped to restore his spirits. He remembered Unzen's practical teaching that had shown him how to do just one thing in its own time with full attention, so that one action flowed into another. Each thing in its own time, without daydreaming or wandering through the tunnels of the mind. Each thing with focus, clarity, simplicity. It was a good practice to resort to when one's mind and heart were troubled.

When he had finished eating he made all good again. He cleared up all he had used and put things back in their places as he'd found them. He had no intention of staying at the Hermitage now that Unzen was gone from it. But he wanted to leave it as Unzen had left it. All in good order lest someone should pass by and wish to stay there, or perhaps even take up residence. It crossed his mind briefly to stay at the hermitage himself for longer, since he had no immediate intentions. But he felt life pulling at him. He was young and this was now no place for someone of his age, at his stage. Besides, when the provisions ran out he would have no means of livelihood. No, he must push on somehow and find a direction, a purpose, for himself.

It is sometimes the case, especially when young, that to travel, to take one's body through time and space, may be a good temporary solution to having no fixed purpose. As one travels one observes the world. And as one observes the world one can find oneself speculating as to one's ideal place within it. And by moving through the world one increases the chance that something may in due course turn up. This may be something good or yet something bad. But whatever it turns out to be, it will of course give rise to something further. And eventually one may find oneself in a better place, a suitable place for the present. It was with this intuition that Ryo packed up his bundle, made provisions for the road, picked up his staff and said farewell to the Hermitage on Cold Mountain. He set off down the trail that had first brought him there, but going this time in the other direction, unresolved as to where he might ultimately be headed. As he set off, he remembered Daremo's poem. Murmuring the words, he realized they still applied to his situation most pertinently.

'Behind me the narrow trail has fallen away,
eroded by rough weathers.
Before me my way is unclear, shrouded in thick
mist.
Therefore I pick my way steadily, step by step,
breath by breath, along the uncertainty of this
winding mountain path.'

It was not long before he was on a main route that connected village to village in this part of the realm. Instead of taking a turn that would have led him back to his own home village he took a different way that led west. This was simply on an instinct which told him it was not right to return home just yet, that such a move would constitute failure, that there was more to be learned, though he could not precisely express quite how. A part of him did yearn at times for home, for the sweet, old familiarity of his childhood, his family, the hut, the pottery with its smells and atmosphere and the sound of known voices, his father's, his mother's, his sister's. But he sensed there was ground for him yet to cover. He would go back some time, he must eventually, but not until he was clear about his destiny. He felt sure there was a core of rightness about his instinct. There were roads still to be travelled for him, he felt, even though he could not predict what they might be.

In due course his belly told him that food would be helpful. As he had provisions packed in his bundle he made his way up a grassy slope and sat down under a small tree to enjoy a small simple meal of rice cake and dried plum. He was about to unpack his food when he saw a figure coming round the dusty road the same way he had come. It looked to be an elderly woman dressed very simply, wearing a straw hat with wide brim and dark, shabby robes. She had a bundle slung over her shoulder and she carried a staff which seemed to be more to support her walking than to use as a weapon. There was something about her, perhaps her appearance, her gait, her age, that reminded Ryo of the poet he had recently met. So Ryo paused to watch the woman making her way along the dusty track towards him.

It was just then that around a bend in the road ahead, beyond which the view was screened by the grassy bank on the other side of the track, a large man came. He was hairy, unkempt and had a lumbering gait. He had the evident strength of a man in middle age. A sturdy man. And there was an air of threat, of menace, about him. Ryo felt a sense of alarm for the elderly woman approaching him, though she simply continued towards him on her way.

Who was it that the sturdy man reminded Ryo of? Something about him jogged Ryo's memory. That was it, the brigands! The ones who had come to Ryo's village when Ryo had first encountered Akio. The story from Akio had been that Hayato the Falcon was ridding the realm of lawlessness, that there would be few brigands now remaining. Most would have been flushed out and executed by Hayato's militia. But perhaps one or two remained, no longer bearing obvious weapons but carrying staves that could be used as such, and appearing like ragged beggars or itinerants in order to pick off vulnerable victims for food, money or anything of value?

Ryo's speculations were soon answered. The sturdy man had blocked the old woman's path, unaware of Ryo's still presence beneath the tree up the bank. Ryo could just make out his words.

'Old woman,' said the rogue, 'you will not pass until I've had whatever I can find of use from you. Food, money, or anything I can sell. Hand over and I'll let you pass unharmed. Resist or refuse and . . .' He raised his staff in a threatening manner, as if to show he would whack the poor woman about the head with it. It was at this point that Ryo intervened.

'Stop!' Ryo's voice rang out from up the bank.

Taken aback, the villain lowered his staff and looked about him. He was surprised to find he had an audience, thinking himself to have been quite alone with the old woman. It took him a moment to pick out the figure of Ryo descending swiftly from the bank up to his left. It took him a little longer to discern the person approaching was simply a youth, alone and unarmed, apart from the walking staff he was holding. Still, this was an unwanted interruption of his robbery and would have to be dealt with first. The rogue was annoyed at the complication of what had seemed like an easy picking. He turned angrily on Ryo, ready to give him a good whacking for his intervention.

But Ryo stood his ground, looking him directly in the eye and addressing him with clear confidence. 'Be on your way, man. Let this woman pass in peace. Are you not ashamed to pick on a poor elderly traveller?'

The villain's face shifted from sheer surprise to an expression of extreme annoyance and then fury. He raised his staff and swung it straight at Ryo's head with sufficient force to stun if not kill him.

But Ryo ducked the blow and almost instantly drove the end of his staff with full force into the man's chest. The man had great bulk, but the blow surprised him and took his breath away. Ryo followed by twisting his staff and delivering a sharp sideways swing at the man's left ankle. *Crack!* The man winced and then roared with pain and anger. He dropped his staff, allowing Ryo to seize his moment. Ryo slipped his staff through the gap in the man's legs and then pushed on the end he was holding as if it were a lever. The man's right leg lifted from the ground and as Ryo lunged towards him he was only supported by his damaged ankle. He toppled backwards like a statue and fell heavily to the ground such that all the breath was expelled from his body. Ryo swiftly kicked the man's staff out of reach and was upon him holding his staff like a spear with one end pressing into the man's throat. It seemed possible that a sharp thrust might even kill the rogue. But this was merely a threat, not an intention.

Ryo drew breath and spoke quickly. 'If you're to rob poor travellers in future, then learn to use that stick of yours with more skill. But far better, find an honest way to earn your food. Have you not heard? Emperor Hayato has rid the land of villains like you, for the most part. You're a dying breed. There's no place for the likes of you in the new world. And there are fighters like me to see you off. Be careful. We shall leave you here. Don't think to follow us or next time I'll not be so compassionate with you. And be warned I am one of many. We don't look impressive but you've tasted how we fight. So mend your ways.'

He turned to the old woman. 'Don't worry, mother, I'm going your way. I'll accompany you. This won't happen again, but to be on the safe side let me travel alongside you. I would enjoy the company. Let me fetch my bundle from under that tree and we can leave. This rogue will take a while to be back on his feet but he'll survive. He may be limping for a while but there's nothing he won't recover from. Hopefully he will change for the better, but that's his affair, I think.'

It was true. The beaten rogue lay there, gathering his breath before attempting to stand up again. It took barely a minute for Ryo to fetch his own bundle and rejoin the old woman on the road. Once he was back the old woman nodded and the two new companions set off. Ryo paused at the bend in the road to see the villain standing and rubbing himself before beginning to limp away in the other direction, using his staff as a walking support.

To begin with the old woman and Ryo walked along in silence. Ryo was a little dazed still from the unexpected encounter. He was also aware that this was the first time he'd ever used his learned skills in genuine single combat. He had thought himself barely trained at all, but in this contest he had clearly got the better of his adversary. He had learned more than he'd realized.

The old woman spoke. 'You are an unusual youth,'

she commented. 'Not many lads your age could do such a thing.'

'Oh,' replied Ryo with genuine modesty, 'I am hardly trained at all. I have little skill compared to others.'

'Most people have no skill in such things,' said the woman. 'The little you say you know gives you great advantage in combat, I think.'

'Well,' replied Ryo, 'I am glad it was enough to save you from harm or robbery, or both, mother. It is good to have such skill as I have put to proper use for once.'

'Yes,' said the woman. 'Fighting is too often put to bad use. It was heartening to see it used to positive effect.'

Ryo noticed that the old woman seemed unperturbed. She had just been threatened with robbery and violence yet was talking in terms of general good rather than her own personal safety. Was this not a little odd? Ryo became curious about his new companion and looked at her sideways. She was looking straight ahead and walking steadily. Her gait was firm and even. She did not appear to be an old woman who had just been through an unnerving experience.

It was then that Ryo remembered he had been about to eat. The rush of the sudden combat had taken all appetite out of him for a while, but now things were settling he began to feel his hunger again.

'I was about to eat when you were threatened,' he

said to the old woman. 'Would you stop and eat with me up here on the bank?' he enquired, pointing.

'I carry no food with me at present,' the old woman replied. 'But I'll sit with you and talk, if you wish. I am not so far now from my home. I am returning there from a visit.'

'Share my food with me,' said Ryo. 'It's very plain, but it's solid and wholesome,' he added.

'That is kind,' the old woman said. 'First one act of service and then another. You are generous.'

Ryo nodded modestly and they went to sit up on the grassy bank overlooking the road. Ryo unpacked his food and the two began to eat quietly. As they ate Ryo took his flask out of his bundle and put it between them. It was fresh stream water from Cold Mountain.

They sat and ate quietly at first, occasionally reaching down to drink from the flask, but looking straight ahead of themselves at the open road. It was quiet. Nobody passed by and nobody could be heard or seen approaching from either direction.

When the old woman had finished eating she sat in silence for a minute or so, then she spoke. 'Thank you for the food,' she said plainly. Then she added, 'You have the air of a troubled young man. Tell me about yourself.'

For a moment Ryo paused uncertainly. Who was this woman? Where was she from? How much could Ryo tell her? Would it be safe to do so? What of Ryo's connections to the Hidden Ones? Could he reveal such things in a world that had done its best to stamp them out? How could he tell his story without including any incriminating material?

Ryo looked closely at the woman's face. His intuition told him that this was not the face of an informer or a spy. There was a genuine sincerity about this woman's look and manner that put Ryo at his ease. He felt himself wanting to know her better. There was something soothing about being in her company. In certain ways she reminded Ryo of Unzen.

So Ryo told his story. He began with the arrival of the brigands in his home village, so long ago now, it seemed. Then he went on to tell of his journey to Cold Mountain in search of the 'Hermit'. He described his training with Unzen and his subsequent apprenticeship at the Hill Camp. Then he went on to relate the dark episode of the annihilation of the Hidden Ones and the devastation of the Hill Camp. At this point he saw the old woman's face grow serious. Ryo heard her let out a low sigh. And finally he told her of the climb up Cold Mountain and the encounter with Unzen's corpse. He even risked telling the strange experience of riding the dragon. He sensed that his listener would not judge him as mad or deranged provided he told it plainly, just as it was, without justification or apology.

When he had finished telling his story Ryo broke

off and sat quietly, waiting for some response from his listener. For a while she stayed silent, as if digesting all that she'd been told. Then slowly she began to speak.

'You have been through a lot,' she said. 'Not many so young have seen such things. There must be much weighing on your mind, on your heart, right now.'

Ryo nodded. 'Yes,' he said simply. Then he added, 'Much of the time my thoughts are full of what has happened and my mind is full of images of what I have seen. It is as if I keep re-entering bad dreams. But I know the dreams to be real. All these things, I know, have occurred. The deaths, the losses, the changes. They are recent and true.'

The old woman suddenly changed tack. 'Where are you going to next?' she asked directly.

'I have no destination,' replied Ryo frankly. There seemed no point in concealing the truth from the old woman now that he had told her so much already. It might normally appear deranged or foolish to be travelling without an end in sight, but that was precisely Ryo's intention. To see what would turn up. So he resumed, 'I do not know where to go next. I am not ready to return home yet. It would seem like failure, I feel. I am travelling to see what turns up. I may try to find work somewhere, on a farm or in a village, in return for my keep. I simply need to keep myself alive until I know what to do with myself, until I find some convincing purpose.

'The purpose I had has been plucked away and in view of what has happened I think I have lost the appetite I had for the Way of Fighting. That way seems only to lead to death and loss. It's true I fought just now for a good reason. I could not have done that had it not been for my training. So I'm grateful and glad that I could step in like that and protect you. That is a good thing. But a life given over to fighting, to martial ways, to war . . . I see now that such a life may not be the best way for one such as me to take. Akio tried to tell me that when we first met. Perhaps he read me straight away. Perhaps he had the wisdom to see through my boyish zeal. That would not surprise me. He was a great fighter but I think he must also have had great heart, great mind, great soul and also some wisdom, since he was Unzen's star pupil in his training. I think it turns out he was right . . . And yet I do not, I cannot, regret the paths I took that led me from my village. Terrible things have happened and I have lost almost all my friends, my community. But somehow I know I needed to do what I did. It was not wrong to go to Cold Mountain to find Unzen. It was not wrong for me to study at the Hill Camp. How strange that it was right yet wrong at the same time. I am rambling, I know, yet this is the way my thoughts, my feelings, run

at the moment. I am simply trying to find my way . . .'
He broke off and looked down at the grass. He noticed
a small snail making a slow, steady progress up a slant-
ing blade of grass. It reminded him of a short poem his
father had taught him about such a thing, the snail's
slow ascent being like our passage through life, or our
progress on a particular quest. Then he came back into
the present where the old woman was sitting quietly
next to him on the bank. He felt a sudden rush of
gratitude towards this old person who had sat and
listened so patiently and receptively to his tale of
woes. The old woman had not interrupted nor tried
to dissuade him from any opinions or feelings he'd
expressed. She had simply sat and listened, as if quietly
absorbing and collecting all that Ryo had to say.

But now the old woman was turning towards him
and starting to speak. 'Come and stay with me for a
while,' she suggested. 'I can offer you simple accommodation and food. You will find my home basic and
sparse, but you will be warm and dry at nights and you
will not be hungry. We can talk if it helps, and I may
be able to give you some kinds of advice, perhaps. But
mostly you will have time to settle your spirits, to calm
your mind and to begin to choose a direction for yourself. There are occasions in life where one can benefit
from a time of pause and reflection. Such time is not
always available. But in return for your services today,

and in response to your situation as a young person undecided, I make you this offer. Will you accept? Can you see a point to such an idea?'

Ryo did not have to think long. The old woman reminded him somewhat of Unzen. This in itself was a comfort. The old woman's manner, her behaviour, was reassuring. She seemed steady and calm. To stay with such a person for a while could prove soothing. And besides, Ryo had no idea of where he might otherwise sleep that night, or where his next meals would be coming from. He would aim to be a helpful and considerate guest. Perhaps there would be ways he could earn his keep with the old woman until such time as he had a clearer idea of what to do next.

So Ryo said, 'Yes, mother. Thank you. That is kind. I would like that very much. I accept your offer.'

'Good,' replied the old woman. 'My name is Yuzuki. My home is only an hour or so from here on foot. Shall we set off now?'

'Yes,' said Ryo. 'And I am Ryo, son of the potter Takumi from Furukawa, the village of the Old River.'

At the mention of Ryo's father and Furukawa, Yuzuki cocked her head with interest and nodded. Perhaps she knew the place? But she said nothing further and began to make her way down the bank to the dusty road.

As they walked they talked from time to time. They talked in spells and then lapsed into easy silences while both were with their own thoughts. But every now and then one of them began to speak again, either to ask a question or to resume a topic they had been discussing.

At one point Ryo asked, 'Do you mind me enquiring? Am I being too personal? But what is it you do? Do you have a trade or a profession? What has been the nature of your life?'

Yuzuki was not troubled by this direct questioning. She nodded easily and said simply, 'I am a kind of priest. That is a way of putting it. As a young woman I trained at the Temple of Sighing Pines. I lived and practised there many years and was eventually asked to be Abbess at Full Moon Temple, a cousin settlement to Sighing Pines. In due course I was allowed to set up my own hermitage that we are heading for now. This is the way in the temples. When you get to a certain age you earn the right to go solo as a hermit-priest. This means you can make your own settlement, where you live and practise into old age, returning to the temple community if you become infirm and unable to care for yourself at the very end of life. But during your time as a hermit you form links to the nearby villages. Then people come to you for advice, help, guidance and such. And some come to learn meditation that will help them in their daily lives to remain steady and grounded. In return they bring alms, gifts of food and drink, which helps me survive as a hermit, though I grow some of my own food too. And if things get thin, I can apply to the temple for assistance. The temple is run like a large farm, so the members work on it to produce food. Some members do fine craft work, pottery, calligraphy, painting and poetry or making bamboo flutes, the subtle ones called *shakuhachi*. What they make is bought by patrons and some is sold at markets in towns. So you see the temple communities earn their keep to a great extent, as they do not wish to be seen as a burden on the people. People who live near the temples use them, also, as places to go to for advice and support when they are troubled or worried or beset by anxieties around the meaning of their lives. Some people call that "spiritual" advice, but I prefer, like many of my order, not to use that word . . .'

She paused there for a moment so Ryo interjected, 'Why so? Why not?'

'In my order, that some call Ch'an,' said Yuzuki, 'we learn to see beyond distinctions between spirit and matter. Spirit and matter come to be seen as two sides of the thinnest sheet of paper you might imagine. They are entirely interfused and cannot exist without each other. So I would say that my own being is both spirit and matter interpenetrating, if you can imagine that. But I am using thoughts and words to describe some-thing that in my order is explored more through direct experience. I am using thoughts and words to talk to you about my order, simply to give you a flimsy, initial sketch of our way seen from the outside. To understand our ways fully you need to practise and to live the Ch'an way. We tend to be suspicious of words and concepts as a vehicle for teaching the kinds of experience we explore. This can make us seem strange to some, but there is a sound purpose to it that you tend only to "get" with consistent application of our methods. As a hermit I have a few pupils who come from the villages to learn these methods. They practise at home when they can and they come me from time to time for further instruction. If you stay with me you may meet them when they come.'

She fell silent for a while so Ryo nodded and said 'Ah . . .' to register that he had heard. Then he dropped back into his own thoughts.

As he turned over what Yuzuki had just said to him he found himself reminded yet again of Unzen. But Yuzuki was a priest, a kind of holy woman, while Unzen followed the way of fighting. How strange that the two people's ways were so alike. He could see in Yuzuki a similar steadiness, firmness, calmness that Unzen had shown. And, now Ryo looked back on it, Yuzuki had seemed strangely unshaken by her encounter with the villain. True, Ryo had stepped in before seeing what Yuzuki might have done in response to the villain's threat. But most people would have shown more shock, fear and even subsequent alarm at such a happening. It seemed unlikely, though not impossible, that Yuzuki would know how to fight effectively. But her manner, her deportment and even some of the content of her speech were powerfully reminiscent of Ryo's old master, Unzen. Ryo felt drawn to Yuzuki. He began to feel that there might be helpful things to learn from her. The intuition that had led him to set out for an unknown destination was beginning to seem valid.

Chapter Seventeen

When they arrived at Yuzuki's hermitage Ryo noticed immediately how it reminded him of Unzen's home at Cold Mountain. Yet Yuzuki's settlement was even more ordered. There was a little weeding to be done in the vegetable plots but that simply reflected Yuzuki's absence of a day or so during her visit away. But the whole place, while simple and made from basic, poor materials, had a kind of quiet dignity which immediately caught Ryo's attention and held him in its spell. This would indeed be an ideal place to rest awhile and gather his thoughts and perhaps some peace of mind. Maybe here he could start to plan for the future.

As Ryo looked at Yuzuki's main hut a phrase came into his head. What was it his father would have called this? Yes, that was it, 'wabi-sabi'. *Wabi-sabi*, his father had explained, expressed the idea of a kind of refined poverty. Simple and poor, yet dignified. Not requiring luxury or overt elegance in order to claim refinement. But bearing refinement within in such a way that it shone through the simplicity it wore on the outside. His father sought to achieve a quality like that in his work, in the pots and ceramic wares he made back in Furukawa.

Yuzuki's voice cut across these thoughts. 'I will make tea for us. That is a good way to begin.'

Ryo caught that slightly odd word 'begin' that Yuzuki had used. Begin? Begin what? It sounded almost as if Ryo was about to embark on some process, some task, some endeavour, rather than simply coming to stay for a while with this old woman. But Ryo reminded himself that Yuzuki had an original, an idiosyncratic way of expressing herself so that perhaps he was reading too much into a simple turn of phrase.

They put down their bundles in the small lobby and he noticed that Yuzuki, having taken off her sandals, made a small bow before entering the main space. Ryo, well trained by Unzen in the art of learning by imitation, did the same. Yuzuki took her seat on a cushion beside some tea making equipment and beckoned to Ryo to sit likewise on the cushion opposite, one of several provided for guests. As Ryo watched, Yuzuki then rose to fetch fresh water from outside and to create fire with a small tinder box. This took a while, so Ryo simply sat quietly, as he had learned to do with Unzen, letting his attention focus on his breath and allowing thoughts and feelings to come and go as they would. He felt comforted to be here and he felt safe. For the first time since leaving the Hill Camp with Akio and the Hidden Ones he felt he could relax into himself and lower his guard. He knew he could trust Yuzuki to do him no harm and he sensed already that the old woman had an interest in his wellbeing.

In due course Yuzuki returned with some glowing coals of charcoal and a small metal pot for heating water. She set the coals and added a few more and placed the pot to hang just above the heat. Then she turned to a small cupboard within reach and took out a ceramic teapot and two tea bowls. As Ryo saw them he gave a small gasp.

'Yes,' responded Yuzuki. 'They are very fine ware, are they not?'

'But those were made by my father!' said Ryo with astonishment and rising emotion.

'Ah, so you recognize them?' said Yuzuki with a smile.

'Of course. I used to help him in the pottery at Furukawa before I left to find Cold Mountain,' Ryo gabbled. 'I would know his work anywhere. Some pieces I helped with myself, even.'

'Your father is a very fine potter,' said Yuzuki. 'None of the members who potted at Sighing Pines were his equal. His work has gathered reputation over the last few years. I have never met your father, but these pieces were a gift from Full Moon when I left to set up my hermitage here. Someone there had travelled to his pottery to buy pieces, having heard of his work. These were bought specially, as a gift for me.'

For a moment Ryo felt himself swell with pride. This was his father, his father's work, being praised by a person of understanding. He felt a kind of glow at being of the same family, of having a special connection to these fine pieces of ware. Yes, for a moment he felt special and singular. And he also felt a sense of belonging, a sense of his origin, of where he had come from. It was a good feeling. Suddenly his thoughts turned to Chou, his only friend left alive. She was less fortunate in her family. As far as she knew they were poor peasants who scraped a living from the land and who had rejected and abandoned her because she was a girl. Ryo suddenly acknowledged how fortunate he had been in his family, in their love and their stability. And not least in their accomplishments.

Now Yuzuki was talking to him again. 'I recognized your father's name when you mentioned who you were and where you came from, as we set out on our journey here. But I did not want to distract you. You seemed unsettled and I thought it better to let you talk as you needed to, or not at all, without undue pressure from me. So now I know a little more about you. You say you used to work with your father in his pottery. He was presumably training you in the art himself. Was he disappointed, do you think, when you left for Cold Mountain to learn the arts of fighting?'

'I can't say, really,' said Ryo. 'He was very generous to me about it. He said there was no use in forcing a young person into something against their will. And I, of course, could only think then of becoming like Akio, who I had been so impressed by when he showed such skill with the brigands. I think, maybe, he may have been disappointed, somewhat, now I reflect. But I was younger then and too full of my own designs to think about it.'

'Ah,' sighed Yuzuki. 'The old and the young. It is ever the way.' She smiled and shook her head, but more with acceptance than with disapproval or sadness. 'Let us have tea now.'

The water had boiled and Ryo watched as Yuzuki with great skill sprinkled the green powder into the bowls, filled them with boiling water and then whisked the mixture briskly with a light bamboo whisk. She then passed one to Ryo who took it with his right hand, cupping his left hand beneath it to steady it and avoid spillage. He then placed it on the ground in front of him. Yuzuki did the same with her own tea bowl. They both paused. Ryo had been trained by his father in the art of being a guest at a formal tea ceremony. Since his father made the ware for the ritual he had thought it only fitting to teach his son how such things were correctly used.

'Listen,' said Yuzuki raising one finger toward the roof of the humble shack. As Ryo listened he could hear the drip of water from the bamboo guttering landing in the water butt beneath it. As he listened intently it was as if the sound cut right through to his innermost being. He closed his eyes for a moment so that it was as if all there was in the universe was this tiny but reverberant sound. And then he could distinguish a faint breeze alongside it, gently rustling the leaves of the bamboo grove outside. In the distance, sharply and suddenly, came the cry of the hototogisu, the cuckoo bird whose call echoed from time to time through the hills and forests of Chazan.

This is like being with Unzen, thought Ryo. Only with Unzen I was taught to listen in order to sift out sounds of incipient danger. Here, in the tea ceremony, I am being encouraged to listen just to listen. Instead of listening acutely for a purpose I am being invited to listen just for its own sake, simply to be in the present and to savour that experience for itself.

He knew enough to play his part in the ceremony, but he had never really participated in such an event in an authentic way. This was a new experience for him. When he lifted the tea bowl to his lips and sipped the fresh, bitter, green brew he felt awakened by it. The hot liquid seemed to sharpen his senses and draw him into a higher state of awareness, but not away from the world, rather into a fuller and richer engagement with it.

'This is my first formal tea ceremony,' Ryo said quietly.

'Ah,' Yuzuki nodded. 'You seem to know the etiquette though . . .'

'Yes. My father taught me when telling me about tea wares,' said Ryo. 'He would have taught me more had I stayed at home to be a potter like him.'

'Well,' said Yuzuki quietly, 'all things in their time. You can pick up now where you left off. First you were potting. Then you were fighting. Now you are just sitting . . . and drinking tea.' She smiled, half to herself.

In due course Yuzuki prepared them each a second cup of tea. When it was poured and they were settled again she gestured gently to Ryo's left. Ryo turned to look at the *tokonoma*, the alcove where a scroll hung on the wall and where beneath, on a pedestal, stood a vase in which there was an arrangement of twigs with small buds not yet broken open. He knew of such alcoves, for Unzen had maintained one in his hut on Cold Mountain, and there was one in his family home and in other homes in Furukawa. Mostly such scrolls bore a simple piece of calligraphy, a word or phrase written in ink brush with as much skill as the writer could manage.

Occasionally it might be a picture showing a landscape or rustic scene. But here the calligraphy was just a circle, a large, apparently swiftly drawn circle, as if the calligrapher had swept their brush deftly round in one move to leave behind the trail of their action.

'Do you know the "enso"?' asked Yuzuki politely. 'Have you seen one before?'

'No . . .' said Ryo thoughtfully. He found it strange that such a simple motif could seem to emanate such power. It was curiously arresting, this plain circle that showed the dash of the brush with its thick, black ink.

'This *enso* is reputed to be the work of Kanzan, the wild poet of Cold Mountain. I cannot verify this for sure, but it is indeed a fine example of *enso*. It has great power and depth. This was a calligrapher of true understanding.'

'Is Kanzan still there on Cold Mountain?' asked Ryo. 'I never saw nor heard of him while I was there.'

Yuzuki smiled. 'Oh, Kanzan died about fifty years ago, but his reputation survives. He left poems and calligraphy behind. Some found their way to Full Moon Temple where I was able to read them. That is how I know of him. He was a wild outsider as a person, but in many ways his understanding of Ch'an was strong. The Ch'an priests were uneasy about him as he did not behave properly by their own standards. But he used just to laugh at them and tell them they should loosen up. He was a good lesson, really, I think. He reminds us there may be more than one way to crack an egg.'

As he listened to Yuzuki talking Ryo again felt grateful to life and to chance for throwing the two of them together. First Akio, then Unzen, now Yuzuki. They were all people, human beings, in their own right. People with their own lives and histories. Yet to Ryo they already stood like signposts in his own life, forces that influenced him and directed his progress. Yuzuki he had only just met, of course, but Ryo could already sense that the old woman would be of importance to him.

Over the following days Ryo found that he could relax into himself and begin to think about his future. He found being with Yuzuki comforting, reassuring but also interesting. And although Yuzuki reminded him of Unzen, she seemed somehow even more poised, more grounded, more steady. It was hard for Ryo to find the right words to describe what he perceived in Yuzuki's manner, and even there it was not so much a question of 'manner' as a sense of her very 'being'. Her movements were fluid. Whenever she performed a task she seemed to do it with unforced attention and usually with practised ease. Seeing her go about her business struck Ryo as rather like watching water flow, the way it did in the stream below his father's pottery at Furukawa.

Ryo helped with various tasks that needed doing. He

asked Yuzuki at the outset if he could help with practical things, rather than being an 'idle guest'. He helped by weeding the vegetable plots. He washed dishes and pots when they had eaten. He prepared food alongside Yuzuki, who had the skill of making the simplest of foods delicious by the way she lightly cooked them and seasoned them with wild herbs, which she gathered in the vicinity, and cultivated herbs, which she grew in her own plot.

In spare moments Ryo took the path up the hill to sit at the top and take in the view of the surrounding villages in the gently undulating landscape where Yuzuki's hermitage was set. Up here, above the hermitage, under the open sky with a view of the nearby world, Ryo found he could reflect on all that had happened since he left his home to seek the Hermit on Cold Mountain. Over and over he let the story play through his mind so that little by little the painful parts of it, while still imbued with sadness, could be held in his consciousness without provoking extreme grief, tears or distraction. He spoke to Yuzuki about this, who advised him simply to allow the process to do its work.

'Time,' said Yuzuki, 'is of the essence here. Allow time,' she prompted, 'to have its effect.'

Ryo knew this was right, as it was what he was beginning to experience from day to day.

Also he sat with Yuzuki. Yuzuki would sit in

meditation several times a day, and also at random when she appeared to have nothing else to do. Ryo had learned to sit in this way with Unzen, in the context of his martial training, but here Yuzuki guided his sitting towards a slightly different mindset.

'If you want to sit *zazen*, the Ch'an way,' she explained, 'then you are not sitting to prepare for anything or to achieve anything but simply to be where you are entirely. That sets up "being where you are" as an objective, which of course it cannot be, if you think about it. If you are intending to be where you are then clearly you are not there, if you take my meaning. But these are just words. Better to do it regularly and let the experience perform its work.'

'This seems very close to what Unzen told me,' Ryo thought aloud, 'but it seems to have a different spin, a different angle or twist to it, I think.'

'I can see you already know how to use the breath to settle yourself,' said Yuzuki. 'And also how to use the breath as a kind of anchor or ballast. But once you are sitting with good focus you can drop the attention on the breath and simply sit. If thoughts, feelings or sensations occur to you in that state, do not push them away, but also do not latch on to them or follow them. Let them come and go as the clouds pass over the hilltop where you sit each day. Watch them with that watching part of your consciousness that can observe without getting caught up in them. If you find yourself getting in a tangle with them you can always return to the breath, which is ever a reliable spine to support your sitting. You can think of the breath as the mast to hold on to during the whirling storm of thoughts and emotions . . .'

Ryo used this advice and day by day began to find his sitting a great help in his recovery.

'Wherever you are,' said Yuzuki, 'whatever circumstances you find yourself in, this practice is there with you as a resource. So long as you have breath in your body and air around you, then you have this to steady yourself, though there is more to it than self-steadying in the long run. I cannot say what, though. That's for you to find out for yourself, if you will . . .'

Days passed and a gentle rhythm established itself for Ryo. Rising from sleep, sitting *zazen* with Yuzuki, preparing food, taking tea, gardening and attending to domestic chores. And when no further tasks presented themselves, taking the walk up to the hilltop to be with himself and his thoughts about his past and his immediate future. From time to time visitors came to see Yuzuki and sometimes Ryo would be invited to sit with them as question and answer passed between visitor and Yuzuki. Sometimes visitors came singly or in twos or threes for meditation instruction and, similarly, Ryo would be invited to sit with them in order to benefit from the sessions, which he did. Occasionally, too, Yuzuki would ask Ryo to go on an errand for her, sometimes to deliver a message to a nearby village, sometimes to fetch provisions they needed, and Ryo would relish these small tasks as they took him out into the surrounding areas he had seen from his hilltop.

It was a good time and several weeks passed like this. Gradually Ryo became aware of feeling stronger in himself, as if he were recovering internally from the blows struck by the annihilation of the Hidden Ones and the encounter with Unzen's decomposed and ravaged corpse. He did not forget any detail of those harsh experiences. His memory remained intact. And there was sadness and loss around the incidents. But there was a softening of the sharp, intense and bitter griefs that came with them. They were gradually being transformed from severe traumas to the facts of his past life, the harder facts which, while being difficult to digest, could not be made to disappear and which, slowly, would have to be accommodated by Ryo as episodes in his story.

There came a day when Ryo had been sitting with Yuzuki and Yuzuki had rung the small bell that she used to mark the end of their meditations together. The bell was a small metal bowl that Yuzuki tapped gently with a wooden stick. It gave a sharp, clear *ting* that gradually blended into a kind of undulating tail of sound as it faded away. The sound had a seeming purity to it that had a way of wafting into the mind through the ears, both refreshing and soothing at the same time. It was the perfect way to signal the end of a meditation session.

Sometimes they would sit for a little longer in silence before rising and moving into the next thing to be done. Sometimes one or the other would say something that might start a dialogue between them. Today was such a day and it was Yuzuki who broke the silence.

'You seem much calmer these days than when you first came to stay. It shows in your every movement.'

'Yes,' said Ryo. 'My stay with you has helped greatly. I am beginning to see a way forward for myself, I think.'

'Do you have any particular thoughts about that that you could tell me yet?' asked Yuzuki.

It was unusual for her to press Ryo on anything, but Ryo felt no pressure due to the gentle way in which the question was put.

'I am thinking . . .' said Ryo, slowly at first, '. . . that I would like to visit my family again. Until now I felt unready. I could not return home as a failure, as not having achieved my intentions. But now it feels different . . .'

'How so?' asked Yuzuki.

'Well . . .' said Ryo slowly, 'I've been looking at the vase in the alcove. I don't know who made that. It's not one of my father's, I'm fairly sure. And I've been noticing the tea wares we use for tea ceremony, which are my father's, of course. And I've been gazing at the *enso* on the scroll. And I've been thinking how good it is to make things, to create things of use and of beauty, either or both. And it seems to me that I was blessed to be brought up in the house of a potter, a potter so gifted with skill and with insight. But I think because I was born to it, because it was my home and simply what I knew and took for granted, I could not see it for what it was. And when I saw Akio take on the brigands I was entranced by what I saw. I was seduced by the heroics. I wanted to be a hero like him. He would have refused such a description, of course, but to my younger eyes then that is how he appeared. I could think of nothing but to be such a person, with such abilities and prowess.' He paused, but Yuzuki sat motionless, quietly listening, silently encouraging him to go on.

'Right from the start Akio tried to discourage me,' Ryo continued. 'Back there when I pursued him out of the village he told me, I remember clearly, how fighting was no way for most people to lead a life. How it was sterile, empty and lonely and might result in a short and bitter life. But I could not hear of it then, whereas now I have tasted that bitterness all too fully. And Akio has gone that way himself, even one so skilled and master-ful as him. And I would never have made such a one as he was in his chosen way. Even Katsuo showed far more promise than me back at the Hill Camp. He might have reached Akio's level. And Chou had the better of me with her strange butterfly skills. I was at best mediocre . . .'

'Perhaps as a fighter, as a martial artist singularly,' put in Yuzuki. 'But as a person in your own right, as one who takes up the space allotted to every being, you are as valid as any other. Not many of us can come to be the best at what we do. And even then there may always come along one to better us in due course. Being best is a dangerous aim and a dubious intention. Better to do what calls to us with full engagement and with love.'

Love. Ryo had not heard that word used since he had left home. The word dropped like a pebble into the still pond of his heart sending ripples through his body. Love. The last time he recalled hearing that word was when his mother had said to him, just before he left, 'Remember, Ryo, that you have a family here that love you and that you can always return to, so long as we live . . .'

'So long as we live . . .' The words filled Ryo with a sudden chill of fear. What if something had happened? What if one or all of them had died? What if he returned home to find his childhood swept away by disease, bandits, war or some other disaster? For a moment he imagined the horrors he had experienced visited on his family, on the pottery, on the small, beloved place beside the stream. And he was filled with an urge to leave that very moment, to get up and make haste to his home to make sure that all was safe and intact.

'You look troubled,' said Yuzuki swiftly. 'Has the conversation upset you? Calm yourself. Take a breath. Then tell me your thoughts, if you feel you can.'

Ryo sat for a moment, calming himself as Yuzuki had suggested. Of course it was ridiculous to think of getting up there and then and leaving for home straight away. But an anxiety clung there in him around the idea that something bad might happen to his family before he could get there to see them and be with them. He looked at the anxiety fairly and squarely and breathed into it. It was just an anxiety. To act on it impulsively would do no good. He knew what to do. He simply sat and focused on his breathing, allowing the anxiety to hover there in his consciousness. Gradually it lost its hold on him. Its power reduced like a candle flame flickering out. And then he was back with Yuzuki who sat, typically patient, waiting for him to speak when he was ready.

'I've been wondering whether my father would take me back as his apprentice,' said Ryo. 'To me, now, this no longer feels like failure. I see clearly how to live a life of "making", a good, steady life in which the main purpose is to create, would be a life well lived. As you said, the issue is not one of aiming to become the best and the greatest, but to seek out what calls to us and to aim to do that with full engagement. What was it you said the other day to me about the Ch'an attitude to life? "To function freely in the present time and place with no smallness of mind." I can imagine myself learning to make fine ware at Furukawa in that spirit.'

'To imagine oneself is a start,' said Yuzuki. 'The next step is to begin. And then it's a matter of going on with it. "Going on going on", as they say in Ch'an. It seems to me your stay here has served its purpose. When you came here with me you were a confused and troubled young man. Now you seem steady and you have an intention, an objective. That is all a young person of your age needs in life. The rest is action, for now . . .'

As Ryo heard this, the matter seemed settled. He would head for home as his next move. Whether all would be well there, whether they would still receive him lovingly, whether his father would take him back as an apprentice potter, that would have to be tested. He could only hope all would be well. And, ah, if not, then once more he would have to think again and make further plans.

Was life this hard for all young people? he wondered. Maybe so. But better simply to focus on his own life and to live it, step by step.

He agreed with Yuzuki that he would set off the next day, early enough to get a good day's walking in to see him on his way. He estimated that the journey back would take him several days, to judge from his memory of the journey out, and allowing for the diversion that had led him to Yuzuki's hermitage. Yuzuki spent time with Ryo preparing food that would last a few days. As ever this was done in a quiet, systematic way. Nothing was ever rushed or hurried with Yuzuki. Ryo would not forget this aspect of the old woman.

That night they sat together for the last time. Nothing was said. Decisions had been made and all was in place for Ryo's departure the next day. It was a quiet sitting, though perhaps tinged with a slight air of sadness. They had grown used to each other's company and Ryo knew he would miss the old woman to begin with. Whether Yuzuki would miss him was something Ryo could not guess. He could certainly not ask. It would breach etiquette and correct behaviour. He knew that. But he told himself that Yuzuki might miss him a little for a while. After all, the old woman was human, and, as Yuzuki had told him once, to be wise or enlightened does not release one from human feelings. It simply increases one's chance of managing them more steadily. But there was no question of Ryo staying with Yuzuki indefinitely. It had been quite clear from the outset that the purpose of Ryo's stay was to steady himself until he might be ready to re-enter the world. And now he had reached that point. Yuzuki would be pleased for him that the stay had served its purpose. When Yuzuki rang the bell for the sitting to end they bowed formally to each other from their cushions and retired to bed.

The next day Ryo rose, washed and dressed. Yuzuki had risen ahead of him and was preparing a breakfast of hot millet porridge, salted plums and wheat tea. It would be a good stomachful to start his journey on and Ryo was grateful for the hot, steaming food. He ate it with quiet concentration and then washed his bowl, spoon and cup as ever.

He noticed that Yuzuki had placed his bundle and his sandals by the open door. His staff was balanced up against the wall beside them. The scene made a picture of departure. It would have made a good study for an ink painting, Ryo thought to himself. The open door, the traveller's things, the sandals, the staff. For a moment he stood quietly looking at the scene. He tried to fix it as an image in his mind to remember. It would be a good way to recall Yuzuki's hermitage, which for Ryo had been like a stopping place on his progress. If he were an ink painter he would record it with brush on paper. But he was just a boy, a young man now, who had trained as a fighter but had decided on a better course of life for himself, though this was yet to be tested.

He realized that Yuzuki had moved across the room and was standing formally beside the open door. This signalled to Ryo that it was time for farewell. He went to stand in front of Yuzuki, who looked him directly in the face, in the eyes. She only did this when she was saying something of importance, as if the heart of a message could be transmitted better through ways other than words.

'You know where to find me,' said Yuzuki clearly. 'If things are going well there is no need to contact me, though I would always be happy to hear news of you. If things go wrong or badly for you, feel free to return. Your life is important and I will always be prepared to help you keep it on a good course. That is why I asked you to stay here with me in the first place. I wish you well with your purposes, such as they are at the moment. I know you will think carefully from now about making choices for yourself. This is all I want to say now, apart from . . .' She paused and said the word formally, 'Goodbye.' As she spoke her final word of farewell she bowed a full bow with palms together in front of her.

It was Ryo's turn to speak now. 'Thank you, Yuzuki, for your hospitality and your kindness towards me. I was fortunate to meet you, and staying with you has helped me greatly to steady my mind and soothe my spirits. I feel ready to face the world again and I believe that that was your intention in inviting me to stay with you here in your hermitage. I will never forget you, nor this time here with you. I am grateful for your assistance and advice. When things are clearer for me in my life, when I am on an even way, I shall send word to you to let you know of my progress. Now I must be on my way, I know, so let me simply say, goodbye.'

Like Yuzuki, Ryo made a formal bow which Yuzuki returned, as if echoing him in movement.

Then, silently and with concentration, Ryo put on his sandals, hoisted his bundle over his shoulder, picked up his staff and made his way out of the door and down the path. As he passed through the small wicket gate he turned to fasten it. Yuzuki was standing in the doorway. She had her hand raised informally in a friendly wave. Ryo returned the wave, smiled back at the old woman, then set off on his journey home.

CHAPTER EIGHTEEN

I shall not say a lot about Ryo's journey home. It was much like his journey out, only now he was older and bore the weight of his experiences, so that his feelings as he travelled were altogether different from the mixture of buoyancy and nervous anticipation that had borne him along on his original quest for Cold Mountain and the hermit who turned out to be Unzen.

One small incident, however, is worth reporting before I tell of Ryo's return to Furukawa. It went like this. Ryo was passing through one of the villages on the route home. The village seemed especially familiar to him and he was not sure at first why. It was seeing a man standing in his doorway that brought memory back to him. It was the friendly fellow who had given him tea and rice and a good rest with conversation.

Ryo paused at the man's gate. The man looked at

him curiously as if wondering whether Ryo wanted directions or perhaps was hoping to sell something. Then his face changed to show that he was recognizing Ryo but could not place him.

'Do you remember me?' asked Ryo politely.

Then the man broke into a smile and nodded, 'Ah, yes, now I have it. Aren't you the boy who went looking for Cold Mountain? Oh, yes, and you wanted to meet the Hermit! Did you find him? No, don't tell me yet. Come in and I'll make tea for you and you can tell me all about it . . .'

Ryo hesitated. He was not sure he was prepared to 'tell all about it' to a relative stranger. Besides, some of it might prove dangerous to relate, as he was aware that he might easily be categorized as a survivor of the Hidden Ones. For now he must be judicious as to what he said to whom. If the Emperor had spies out across the land then Ryo might put himself in danger through loose talk of his association with a group that the Emperor had had removed. But hot tea called to him. He would accept the invitation but guard his tongue.

As his host prepared and served the tea Ryo thought of Yuzuki and her formal tea ceremonies. His host was serving tea in the typical way traditional to most ordinary homes in Chazan. It now struck Ryo that this was like the tea ceremony but with the elements of serious focus and aesthetic reflection greatly reduced.

Yet echoes of those were still there, at the heart of the proceedings. Ryo began to realize how much of his country's standard customs bore the influence of Ch'an practice, as if such things had gradually rubbed off on the Chazan way of life over the years.

But now his host was speaking. 'So tell me, did you find your way to Cold Mountain, back then when we first met?'

'Yes,' replied Ryo earnestly. 'I did go there, by following your instructions.'

'And did you find the Hermit, by any chance?' the man pressed.

'Well, I did find someone who might fit that description, indeed,' said Ryo cautiously. 'But that was some time ago. He gave me hospitality so I got to know him a bit . . .' Ryo was treading carefully now. 'I went back later to visit him, though, only to discover that he had died . . .' Ryo managed to mask his grief in saying this, as if he was showing polite sympathy rather than the deep loss he had felt. Due to his time with Yuzuki he had managed to come to terms with some of the most difficult and raw emotions around Unzen's death.

'But was he really a hermit?' pursued Ryo's host. 'And are there others still there?'

'In a way, yes,' said Ryo. 'He *was* a hermit, by most people's understanding. But really he was just a wise old man who wanted to live away from the world towards the end of his life. I think maybe people combined him in their mind with the poet Kanzan who lived on Cold Mountain before him and who died some fifty years ago, I believe. The two characters have become combined in people's minds. I think that kind of thing happens sometimes with rumours and local legends. Certainly it did in my home village.'

'Well, whatever, you have certainly grown and strengthened since I saw you last,' said Ryo's host. 'When you first came to my home you were barely more than a boy, it seems. While now you are a young man, bigger and clearly much stronger. What have you been up to, may I ask?'

'Oh, I found work on a remote farm that the Hermit directed me to. I lived there for over a year and worked hard all that time. That put some muscle on me, I would say.' Ryo thought that that was not too much of an untruth, so felt comfortable with this safe rendition of the facts.

'Well, it is good to move around a bit and to see life when one is young,' said Ryo's host philosophically. 'It can scratch the itch in one's feet and make it easier to settle as one grows older, I suppose.'

Ryo nodded in assent. 'Yes, I am on my way back to my village even now. I hope to find my family safe and well. They may be surprised to see me after so long.'

'And I am sure they will be delighted too,' predicted his host.

Ryo made a brief but courteous farewell, thanking the man for the tea, making it clear he was eager to be on his way in order to cover more miles before dusk. The man was understanding and did not press him for more information, which relieved Ryo greatly.

He bowed by the door then raised his hand in farewell from the gate and strode off through the village leaving the man in his doorway watching him go.

Ryo's journey took him two more days of walking. At night he found safe dry patches where he could roll himself up in his blanket and get enough good sleep to get by on. By now he was well used to this practice. He had also become accustomed to living on minimum provisions while travelling, eking out his scant supplies over the necessary time span and supplementing them with pickings of wild fruit when he spotted it in the hedgerows or edges of woodland along the road. Chazan in those days afforded more wild food than it does now, being then less populated and with smaller villages and fewer towns and so more wild space.

As Ryo drew nearer to his home village he found himself growing excited but nervous at the prospect of seeing his family again. Once more, anxieties arose in him as to their welfare. Would they all be alive and well? Would they be glad to see him? Would they welcome him back? How would his father respond to the idea of him resuming his apprenticeship? But when his thoughts turned so he simply took a deep breath, continued walking and let the anxieties hover in his mind until they moved aside as further thoughts pushed in to take their place.

And soon he was in sight of Furukawa. As he rounded the bend which gave him his first view of his old home village, he paused. Tears came to his eyes, forcing him to stop. He wiped them away with his sleeve and stood gazing at the old place. It seemed as if nothing had changed. There were the familiar rooftops, the dusty road leading through the village, the low hills to either side, the river running along the eastern edge of the houses . . . and the fields and plots where food was grown in the available flat spaces between the hills and beside the road leading into and out of the village. It was all as he remembered it.

He gathered himself and began to walk towards the village. Then he was walking between the houses. As usual, during the early afternoon there were few people about and no one took much notice of him. He had grown and two years had passed, so if anyone saw him they must have read him as a traveller passing through, as so many did on that road from day to day. But now he could see his house, the verandah in front with its awning and its notice offering tea and rice to travellers. He was almost tempted to knock and ask for that to test if he was truly so unrecognizable now. But as he stood looking he saw his mother come out with a mat she probably wanted to shake the dust off. Glimpsing him motionless in the road there she looked curiously towards him for a moment. Then she froze, dropped the mat and came running towards him. This was a most uncommon thing for a woman of her age to do in those days and could only be justified by the pressure of extreme emotion.

'Ryo, Ryo,' she called as she ran, 'is that really you? Are you back at last?' She stopped just in front of him and gazed at him, up and down, taking him in to persuade herself that this was not a vision, that this was indeed her son actually standing in front of her. Then she stepped forward and flung her arms around him letting her head fall onto his neck. He was now taller than her so that this seemed a natural thing to do.

Tears flowed freely between them. His mother took Ryo's face between her hands and looked at it with joy. Then she kissed both his cheeks and his forehead, murmuring, 'Oh, my boy, my lovely boy, you are back, you are back . . .'

And Ryo, gathering his feelings, managed to say in a controlled way, 'Oh, mother, it is wonderful to see you again after so long. I am so glad to find you well and our home still looking safe and secure . . .' But he stopped, for a young girl had just stepped out onto the verandah wondering where her mother had gone so suddenly. Looking in their direction she approached curiously at first then broke into a run when she realized what was taking place.

As she drew near she stopped short and faltered as shyness overtook her. She had not seen Ryo for two years and he was not the young lad she remembered. He seemed more like a young man now, so much had he grown and developed. And she was old enough now, at twelve, to be not quite the child she'd been when Ryo had left. She was just beginning to enter womanhood, so felt a certain restraint towards this new strange young man that was her brother.

'Don't be shy of me, Hana,' said Ryo gently, smiling at her. 'We have both grown and changed, I see. But we need not be so formal in our greeting.' He stepped towards her and drew her into a hug, which she surrendered to. Then Ryo stepped back to take her in, looking her up and down. 'My, you have changed so much in two years,' he marvelled. 'But you are still my little sister, Hana, and I remain your bossy older brother, Ryo, eh?'

She grinned at him shyly and rocked slightly from side to side with happiness and embarrassment.

'But we must call your father,' said his mother suddenly. 'He will be so happy to see you. He is in his workshop even now.'

Hana took this as her task and hurried indoors. Ryo heard her voice calling out from the house, 'Father, Father, come quick. Look. We have a surprise for you. Don't delay. See what has happened.' She did not mention Ryo's name, wanting her father to feel the full effect of seeing Ryo after so long.

Takumi came quickly, wiping his hands on his potter's smock, to see what the commotion was about. When he caught sight of Ryo he stopped, took a deep breath and beamed broadly. He opened his arms wide in invitation and Ryo walked swiftly towards him, locking himself in a firm embrace with his father. After a few seconds they parted and looked each other frankly and clearly in the face, as if assessing their memory of each other and comparing it with their appearance now in this present moment.

'It is wonderful to see you,' said Takumi simply. 'I am so happy that you have come.'

'I hope you were not worried for me,' replied Ryo. 'I admit I feared to find my family not as I'd left them . . . of course, Hana has grown, as have I a bit, but all seems as I remember in Furukawa. There will be gossip and events to relate, no doubt, but it's wonderful to see the old place much as I recall it.'

'I am still making my wares,' said Takumi. 'That has not changed. Only my fame has spread somewhat since you were last here. People come from far and wide to commission work or to see what I have to sell. We are better off than we were. So life has been good to us.'

'I have heard a little of this,' said Ryo. 'I was served tea by a sage, while on my travels. I recognized your work at once and my host spoke highly of your craft. I felt proud of you then, I must say.'

'But speaking of craft and potting, come now to the studio. You have surprised us. Now it is my turn to surprise you . . .' Takumi smiled secretively for a moment.

Ryo, his curiosity roused, followed his father through the house to the studio at the back. Hana and Emi followed behind, whispering.

His father stepped into the familiar setting and turned to face Ryo who looked first at him and then in the direction he was glancing at. A young woman was bending over her work, her face partially obscured. She was just completing a brushstroke which she was apply-ing to a vase that Takumi must have made. She looked up to see why the family had entered the studio. Seeing Ryo her face lit up with evident delight. It was Chou.

'Ryo!' she cried, letting formality drop due to surprise and emotion. 'You have come back at last. I knew you would, but I did not know when.'

'And you have come to my family, as I suggested,' said Ryo with evident pleasure. 'I am so glad you took my words to heart.'

Benches and wares were between them, so, slightly awkwardly, Ryo just bowed to her, hands clasped, while Chou put down her brush and did the same, rising from her seat.

'We must celebrate Ryo's return,' said Takumi. 'Emi, let's make tea and serve cake around the hearth,' he continued. 'And then we can swap stories and bring ourselves up to date, eh?' He addressed this last remark to everyone, looking at each of them with pleasure.

The family were sitting round the hearth. It was set down in the floor as in all traditional houses of the time, a square pit with a charcoal fire at the centre. Everyone sat on cushions, cross-legged on the floor. A kettle dangled above the fire, suspended from a ceiling rafter. Cake had been served and there was tea in their bowls. But this was not a formal tea ceremony, this was a family reunion, lively with chatter and story-telling. Chou was telling Ryo the story of her visit to find her true parents.

'I traced my home village without too much trouble. But when I got there I found myself unwelcome. When I asked about my family I was told they had been wiped out in an epidemic that had passed through the village a few years ago. But, more than that, the villagers were clearly embarrassed and ashamed to meet me, knowing well that I had been an unwanted girl child and had been left out to die. Perhaps some of the people I spoke to had done the same thing to daughters of theirs in the past and felt awkward meeting me, since I am a survivor of that cruel practice. Whatever the case, there was clearly nothing for me there in my village of origin. So I took your advice and came seeking your family . . .'

'And we are so glad she did,' cut in Ryo's father. 'For she brought news of you, that you were alive and that you would in due course come back to see us and maybe stay a while.'

'So do you know some of my story from Chou, therefore?' asked Ryo, looking round at his family.

'I told them you had trained with Unzen, the hermit, and that you had then joined us at the Hill Camp when you were ready. And I told them . . .' She paused and lowered her voice and her eyes. '. . . About the massacre and how we met up back at the desecrated Hill Camp. I told them of those things, so they are aware of the dangers we both narrowly avoided.'

At this point Ryo's mother put her hand on his arm to reassure herself of his safe presence there, as if to convince herself once again that he was not a ghost or a vision.

'And they asked me to stay here with them, at least until such time as you might return, since there was nowhere else for me to go.'

'And hospitality has its rewards, as you will see,' broke in Takumi. 'For it turns out your friend is a natural with the brush.'

'Yes,' said Ryo curiously. 'You were in the studio painting a pot, I noticed. I did not know you had that skill.'

'Not much,' said Chou. 'But at the Hill Camp I learned some calligraphy, just the basics, from one of the elders who was an expert. He taught me to grind ink and mix it, how to hold and wield the brush and how to form some of the basic characters. He also showed me how to paint bamboo and leaves and birds in flight. I loved those lessons. They were like a secret, special time for me, away from all the emphasis on fighting and combat. My teacher, Hotaka, told me I was a "natural", that in his view I had the gift, that I should pursue this further if ever chance might come about.'

'Which is why I am encouraging her to practise in my studio,' said Takumi happily. 'Already she has inspired me to design some new wares which can bear her work. It could be a new line for me, if only she would stay . . .' He looked at her questioningly.

'Well, Father,' said Ryo looking directly at him.

'This brings up something I have been thinking about for a while now. Since my return from the wrecked Hill Camp I have been brooding over what to do with myself, with my life, from this point on. And I have resolved for myself that the way of fighting is not, after all, my true course. While I was with Yuzuki, the priest, I found myself looking at the vase in her alcove, over and over, more and more drawn to it, for its stillness, its poise, its grace, its beauty. And I found myself thinking how to make a thing so fine might be one of the best things to do in this life. Fighting, it is true, can be a great art. And if you were to see Chou in action,' he nodded in her direction, 'you would see how it can even become a graceful dance. But I found myself thinking back to you, in your studio, making your pots and wares, and I remembered watching you as a child, seeing you magically transform a lump of dull clay into a form and shape that vibrated with wonder. And I recalled you saying that I seemed to show a potential to be a good potter, like you, one day. And I came to realize, with Yuzuki's help, though she did not force the notion on me, that it is easy when young to take for granted the setting in which we grow up, and not to appreciate what possibilities and opportunities surround us in our home and our everyday world.' Ryo stopped himself for a moment, as he realized he was not making his point simply and clearly.

'The short of it, Father, is that I am asking you to take me back on as your apprentice potter, to stay here and work with you and to learn my trade properly. Would you allow that?'

His father sat silently, seriously, for what seemed to Ryo a long while. Ryo began to think he was framing a kindly refusal and he felt his heart sinking. But then his father spoke.

'I never thought to hear those words from you, Ryo. I was saddened, it's true, when you chose to go to Cold Mountain to seek out the Hermit. But had I prevented you from leaving, or tried to, it would only have tangled you up more. It seems by letting you follow your dream I have enabled you to come round to finding your true purpose, your best way in life. Please come back by all means. We shall be three in the studio. You, Chou and me. And who knows, in time, your sister, Hana, may show an interest there, but that will be in the future and she may have other things in mind. What do you say, Chou? Now that Ryo wishes to return to the studio as my apprentice, will you too stay on and develop your brushwork? Just think, together, the three of us . . . consider the wares we might produce. Perhaps we will end up making pots for fine folk, eh?' He laughed, aware of sounding outlandishly ambitious. 'But still, seriously, what do you say?'

Chou looked down into the hearth where the

charcoal glowed warmly. She spoke quietly and modestly. 'I think I should like that above all else. If Ryo is to return to the studio then I know I will be happy there. I love working with the brush and I can think of nothing I would rather adopt as a way.' She looked up directly at Takumi who felt almost startled by the keenness of her gaze. 'Yes, Takumi, I accept your offer gratefully.' She turned to Emi next. 'And thank you for accepting me so readily into your family, Emi. I have none of my own and I have been happy here since I arrived. And you, Hana, have already begun to feel to me like a sister. I have been fortunate. I am so happy that Ryo thought to suggest me coming to you. The Hill Camp saved me from death, so long ago. But now my new family has saved me from loneliness.'

For a moment everyone fell silent, moved by Chou's speech and the depth of emotion that had been evident.

'Then let me pour fresh tea, and serve more cake, to celebrate the occasion,' said Emi firmly. 'This is a special and a happy day at Furukawa.'

I am an old man now, but I think I have managed to tell my story. Perhaps I am unpractised as a writer, but if that is so it is because I have spent my life working in clay, not words. So, yes, I am a potter and not a poet. Pottery, not poetry, has been my way. But the main thing for me is to have got my point across, that life is unpredictable and varied and that nothing lasts for ever. As they say, everything changes, and in the long run nothing endures. All is swept away by time. Sickness, old age and death come to all of us in due course. But that is no cause to mourn or to lose hope. The important thing is to live and to love, and, if possible, where possible, to make something good from time to time. It may be something you can see and touch and hold on to, like a pot or a fine garment or a painting. Or it may be something more ephemeral, such as good food, which is made and gone in a short space of time. Or it may simply be the art, the skill, the knack, of making people happy, or cheerful or at their ease.

It does not matter so much what it turns out to be, but I urge you, if you are reading this, whoever you are, to ask yourself, 'What do I make or do that is good, that brings beauty, pleasure or happiness into the world?' And if you can find no answer to that, seek inside yourself to find the seed, the grain, of something that might fulfil that purpose. We cannot all be great artists or musicians, scientists or storytellers. We cannot reckon to be the best at what we do. But we can, each one of us, look inside ourselves to find a leaning, a direction, that suggests to us how we might make something of worth while we are here. Is this not true?

You will surely have guessed by now that I am Ryo and that this is the story of my own life. How else could I have known so much about his thoughts and feelings in order to tell the tale, unless I had made everything up out of general experience and storytelling method? But as I said, pots, not words, were my way. This has been a simple, artless attempt to tell my story while I still have strength and time.

To answer your curiosity, yes, I stayed on with my father and mastered the arts of clay. That is an ongoing thing. One has never finished. There is always something new to learn if you are earnest in your art. And Chou, too, became a fine brushworker. She not only excelled in painting imagery on many of my pots, but also became a great painter and calligrapher, working on scrolls and fine paper. Together we made a name for ourselves as highly accomplished artists.

Hana, would you believe it, took to music. She sang beautifully and became skilled in the bamboo flute, the shakuhachi, *as well as the* samisen, *the stringed instrument with which she accompanied her singing. She wrote several songs that became popular throughout the land. Yes, we did well. We were lucky. We were productive. But most of all, we were happy.*

Chou and I, you must have guessed by now, got married. In due course we had children, a boy and a girl, now grown up and living lives of their own.

Of course, there were sadnesses, chiefly when my dear parents, who were also like parents to Chou, died, first my father and then not long after, my mother. We scattered their ashes on the small stream that flows at the bottom of the slope behind the studio. It's with the image of that stream I would like to leave you.

My father used to sit on the flat stone beneath the willow tree and gaze at that stream. He taught me to do the same and I continued to do so from then on. I still hobble down there when my spirits need soothing. It is like life, that stream, always the same, always changing. Constant, you could say, in its fluency. Shifting on the surface and with weathers, but essentially the same old, familiar stream. Like time expressing itself through water. What more is there to say?

Acknowledgements

The perceptions and practices described in this book have been gathered across my adult lifetime, shall we say the 50 years between the ages of 16 and 66? It would be impossible to trace and record all the read and heard influences on me during so long a period. But the following people, via their writings and recorded sayings, come to mind. I have doubtless left glaring omissions which I will later regret if this goes to print. But here are the ones I can call up in rough chronological order of my encountering them:

Christmas Humphreys, Hermann Hesse, Nancy Wilson Ross, Alan Watts, Philip Kapleau, Daisetz Suzuki, Robert Aitken, Shunryu Suzuki, Taisen Deshimaru, Soko Morinaga, Matsuo Basho, Issa, Ryokan, Han Shan, Rumi, Mary Oliver, Eckhart Tolle, Steve Hagen, Norman Fischer, Thich Nhat Hanh, Vidyamala Burch, Jon Kabat-Zinn, Mark Williams, Danny Penman, Michael Chaskalson, Diana Winston, Deepak Chopra, John Sarno, Georgie Oldfield & Liz Dyde, Howard Schubiner, Oli Doyle, Shamash Alidina, Joelle Jane Marshall, Patrizia Collard, Valerie Mason-John & Paramabandhu Groves, Christophe Andre, HH Dalai Lama, and the many and various teachers and practitioners of Buddhism and of Mindfulness that I've encountered and spoken with over the years. Thank you all for your lives, your work, your teaching and your practices in all their styles and forms. All has helped. None was wasted. It all goes on going on.

And to my editors David Fickling and Anthony Hinton and all at David Fickling Books, Oxford: thank you for seeing the point of it and for helping me bring it to published shape.

Tony Mitton,
Cambridge, 2017